Wildfire, the Red Stallion

and Other Great Horse Stories

Other books in the series
The Good Lord Made Them All
by Joe L. Wheeler

Owney, the Post Office Dog
and Other Great Dog Stories

Smoky, the Ugliest Cat in the World
and Other Great Cat Stories

Wildfire, the Red Stallion

and Other Great Horse Stories

Compiled and edited by
Joe L. Wheeler

Pacific Press® Publishing Association
Nampa, Idaho
Oshawa, Ontario, Canada
www.pacificpress.com

Cover art by Lars Justinen

Designed by Justinen Creative Group

Interior illustrations from the library of Joe L. Wheeler

Printed in the United States of America

Additional copies of this book are available by calling toll free 1-800-765-6955 or by visiting www.adventistbookcenter.com

ISBN 13: 978-0-8163-2154-4
ISBN 10: 0-8163-2154-X

www.joewheelerbooks.com

06 07 08 09 10 · 5 4 3 2 1

Contents

DEDICATION

I was nine years old, living with my missionary parents in Panama, when my dream of someday owning a horse came true. Though the white horse my folks gave me was nothing much to look at and was thin and bony, just having a horse of my own was perpetual music to me. So it is today, looking back through the years to my childhood, it seems right that I dedicate this book of horse stories to the only horse I ever owned, a horse that filled my life with her name,

MUSICA

Introduction

The Changing World of the Horse

Joseph Leininger Wheeler

Horses stand about halfway between dogs' slavish devotion to man and cats' noblesse oblige. They respond best to kindness backed by strength, anchored by consistency. When their trust is betrayed, such a wound rarely ever fully heals. Horses, like elephants, have long memories.

Somewhere between three thousand and five thousand years ago, a great change occurred. *Equus caballus* first appeared on the steppes of Central Asia. Scholars today label this common ancestor as Przewalski's horse (or *E. caballus Przewalski*); it was sandy in color. Eventually, its descendants spread eastward into Mongolia, China, Europe, Asia Minor, Egypt, and the other nations bordering the Mediterranean. In 1519, the Spanish conquistador Hernando Cortez introduced the horse to Mexico, from where it soon spread all over the New World.

As to what the horse has meant to the human race, *Britannica* editors perhaps have articulated it best:

> The relationship of the horse to man has been unique. The horse was man's partner and friend, carrying him above his fellow man on foot and giving him power and speed. It ploughed his field and brought in his harvest, hauled goods and conveyed passengers, followed game and, later, tracked cattle, and carried combatants into battle and adventurers to unknown lands. It has provided recreation in the form of jousts, tournaments, carrousels, and in the sport of riding. The widespread influence of the horse is expressed in the English language in such terms as chivalry, cavaliers, and cavalry which generally connote honor, respect, good manners, and straightforwardness (*Macropaedia*, fifteenth edition, vol. 8, 1088).

Down through recorded history, the horse has been a symbol of nobility and royalty. Both the Scythian kings and the Egyptian Pharaohs revered their favorite horses so much that when these rulers died, their horses were entombed with their masters. In Greek mythology, the man/horse synthesis, called a centaur, signified the oneness of man and horse. Furthermore, the gods were often depicted on well-trained horses. It was unthinkable for a king, general, statesman, or hero to be other than a superb horseman. The same was true for the Romans.

It's fascinating to note how often famous people associated themselves with their horses: Alexander the Great with Bucephalus, the infamous Caligula with Incitatus (the emperor planned to make him a senator!), Richard II with Roan Barbary, the Duke of Wellington with Copenhagen, Cortez with El Morzillo, and Robert E. Lee with Traveller, to name just a few.

Ramon Adams, dean of Old West historians, had a great deal to say about the horse in the settling of the American West. According to the cowboy's unbreakable code, no matter how hungry or weary he might be, the comfort and nourishment of his horse always took precedence over his own. When climbing mountains on horseback, he'd spare his horse by picking the easiest route; when riding on a hard-surfaced road, he'd ride on the softest part of it. If he met a rider on a grade, he always gave the other the inside. A cowboy's string of horses was never broken. If it was, it usually meant he was about to be fired. No horse buster abused horses. When a rider was thrown, if not crippled, he was expected to crawl back on the horse. A good hand never overworked his horse.

A cowman saddled and unsaddled his own horse. Only in a serious emergency would he ever loan his horse to another. To mount another's personal horse, without permission, was considered an insult of the first magnitude. One did not feed another's horse without its owner's knowledge.

If visiting where he was unknown, he must remain on his horse until invited to dismount by his host. On a stranger's land, a rider should stick to the trail. If he met a driven herd, he should remain in his saddle.

The reason horse stealing was grounds for lynching was that one's horse often represented the difference between life or death for the cowboy on the open ranges.

(*The Cowman and His Code of Ethics,* Austin, Texas: The Encino Press, 1969).

The great change

For well over three thousand years, the horse represented the fastest land speed known to man. Indeed, it was as essential to an age's lifestyle as steam, engines, electricity, and computers are in our modern world. All this lasted until well beyond the advent of the horseless carriage. No more significant and wrenching change has our world ever known than the switch from a horse-driven world to a machine-driven one. Speed gradually made the horse obsolete.

As time has passed, however, even in the industrialized world, the horse has made a comeback of sorts. Today, however, except in societies such as the Amish, the horse's role has tended toward entertainment, relaxation, or sport rather than utility.

In times past, the horse may almost be said to have been a male preserve. During the last century, however, that has ceased to be true. Though the male love of horses has continued, the feminine species has drawn even with the male in terms of horse devotion. So much so that rare is the girl who fails to fall in love with horses (whether real, fictional, or both) during that crucial age of a woman's life (between nine and fourteen) during which books and horses form the bridge between childhood and romance with boys and men.

About this collection

In this collection, some of the greatest nature writers of our age have weighed in with memorable tributes to the horse—writers such as Walter Farley, Zane Grey, Will James, Maurice Maeterlinck, Penny Porter, and Ernest Thompson Seton.

Each of the stories is, in a way, an iridescent piece of stained glass contributing to a multidimensional mosaic of horse and the human love affair with the species.

Chances are that never, between two covers, has there appeared a collection quite like this one—stories that reveal as much about the people who love horses as they reveal about the horses themselves. Two stories deserve special notice: Grace Livingston Hill (known primarily as a Christian romance writer) reveals in "The Ransomers" an entirely different dimension, a depth and breadth, that may surprise readers who mistakenly assume they had pigeon-holed her. Quite possibly, it may well be the greatest short story she ever wrote. Though Eleanor Bailey's "Horse Sense" is ostensibly about a horse, undergirding the narrative is another story—a story about a rural doctor who is faced late in life with his greatest temptation. Of all the stories written on the subject of what it means to be a success in this thing called life, this story may very well be one of the greatest of them all.

Generally speaking, most of the stories collected in this book are set in a time period before the "great change" took place. For comparison purposes, a few feature our contemporary world. In these stories we may vicariously revel in the swan song of wild horses—how tragic that most Americans will never again glory in the sight of horses running free in the wild! But, in story, we may.

Even more significant, however, is the opportunity to become acquainted with the essence of the horse as revealed in these stories: its personalities, its courage, its endurance, its loyalty, its fidelity, its dependability, its idiosyncrasies, its intelligence . . .

And above all—its *heart.*

* * * * *

Wildfire, the Red Stallion

Zane Grey

Fiction and fact often blur with Zane Grey, especially where horses are concerned. Often, on expeditions into the wild country of the Southwest, he'd hear true stories about specific horses that would capture his imagination; later he'd weave such horses into his stories and novels, and later yet he would purchase real-life horses that would carry the same names.

Though no single account is acknowledged as the greatest of all his horse stories, this one comes close. It has everything in it—an abducted heroine who has been roped to the back of one of Grey's most famed horses, the White King; her fiancé, Lin Sloane, astride another legendary horse, Lucy Bostil's Wildfire—both protagonists are being pursued by outlaws as well as a wind-driven forest fire. Death appears all but certain as the fire is coming upon them faster than a horse can run. The combination of all these ingredients adds up to one of the greatest horse stories ever written. The setting: the uplands of Utah, near the Grand Canyon.

* * * * *

Wildfire reached the pines. There, down the open aisles between the black trees, ran the fleet gray racer. Wildfire saw him and snorted. The King was a hundred yards to the fore.

"Wildfire! It's come—the race, the race!" called Sloane. But he could not hear his own call. There was a roar overhead, heavy, almost deafening.

The wind! The wind! Yet that roar did not deaden a strange, shrieking crack somewhere behind. Wildfire leaped in fright. Sloane turned. Fire had run up a pine tree, which exploded as if the trunk were powder!

"A race with fire! . . . Lucy! Lucy!"

In that poignant cry Sloane uttered his realization of the strange fate that had waited for the inevitable race between Wildfire and the King; he uttered his despairing love for Lucy and his acceptance of death for her and himself. No horse could outrun wind-driven fire in a dry pine forest. Sloane had no hope of that. How perfectly fate, time, place, horses, himself, and his sweetheart had met! . . .

Tense questions pierced the dark chaos of Sloane's mind. What could he do? Run the King down? Make him kill Lucy? Save her from horrible death by fire?

The red horse had not gained a yard on the gray. Sloane, a keen judge of distance, saw this, and for the first time he doubted Wildfire's power to run down the King. Not with such a lead! It was hopeless . . . so hopeless.

He turned to look back. He saw no fire, no smoke—only the dark trunks and the massed green foliage in violent agitation against the blue sky. That revived a faint hope. If he could get a few miles ahead before the fire began to leap across the pine crests, then it might be possible to run out of the forest if it were not wide.

Then a stronger hope grew. It seemed that foot by foot Wildfire was gaining on the King. Sloane studied the level forest floor sliding toward him. He lost his hope, then regained it again, and then he spurred the horse. Wildfire hated that. But apparently he did not quicken his strides. And Sloane could not tell if he lengthened them. He was not running near his limit, but after the nature of such a horse, left to choose his gait, running slowly, but rising toward his swiftest and fiercest effort.

Sloane's rider's blood never thrilled to that race, for his blood had curdled. The sickness within rose to his mind. And that flashed up whenever he dared to look forward at Lucy's white form. Sloane could not bear this sight; it almost made him reel, yet he was driven to look. He saw that the King carried no saddle, so with Lucy on him he was light. He ought to run all day with only that weight. Wildfire carried a heavy saddle, a pack, a water bag, and a rifle. Sloane untied the pack and let it drop. He almost threw aside the water bag, but something withheld his hand, and also he kept his rifle. What were a few more pounds to this desert stallion in his last run? Sloane knew it was Wildfire's greatest and last race.

Suddenly Sloane's ears rang with a terrible oncoming roar. For an instant the unknown sound stiffened him, robbed him of strength. Only the horn of the saddle, hooking into him, held him on. Then the years of his desert life answered to a call more than human.

He had to race against fire. He must beat the flame to the girl he loved. There were miles of dry forest, like powder. Fire backed by a heavy gale could rage through dry pine faster than any horse could run. He might fail to save Lucy. Fate had given him a bitter ride. But he swore a grim oath that he would beat the flame. The intense, abnormal rider's passion in him, like John Bostil's, dammed up, but never fully controlled, burst within him, and suddenly he awoke to a wild and terrible violence of heart and soul. He had accepted death; he had no fear. All that he wanted to do, the last thing he wanted to do, was to ride down the King and kill Lucy mercifully. How he would have gloried to burn there in the forest—and for a million years in the dark beyond—to save the girl!

He goaded the horse. Then he looked back.

Through the aisles of the forest he saw a strange, streaky, murky something moving, alive, shifting up and down, never an instant the same. It must have been the wind—the heat before the fire. He seemed to see through it, but there was nothing beyond, only opaque, dim, mustering clouds. Hot puffs shot forward into his face. His eyes smarted and stung; his ears hurt and were growing deaf. The tumult was the roar of avalanches, of maelstroms, of rushing seas, of the wreck of the uplands and the ruin of the earth. It grew to be so great a roar that he no longer heard. There was only silence.

And he turned to face ahead. The stallion stretched low on a dead run; the tips of the pines were bending before the wind; and wildfire, the terrible thing for which his horse was named, was leaping through the forest. But there was no sound.

Ahead of Sloane, down the aisles, low under the trees spreading over the running King, floated swiftly some medium, like a transparent veil. It was neither smoke nor air. It carried faint pinpoints of light, sparks, that resembled atoms of dust floating in sunlight. It was a wave of heat driven before the storm of fire. Sloane did not feel pain, but he seemed to be drying up, parching. And Lucy must be suffering now. He goaded the stallion, raking his flanks. Wildfire answered with a scream and greater speed. Except for Lucy and the White King and Wildfire, everything seemed so strange and unreal—the swift rush between the pines, now growing ghostly in the dimming light, the sense of a pursuing, overpowering force, and yet absolute silence.

Sloane fought the desire to look back. But he could not resist it. Some horrible fascination compelled him. All behind had changed. A hot wind, like a blast from a furnace, blew light, stinging particles into his face. The fire was racing in the treetops, while below all was yet clear. A lashing, leaping flame engulfed the canopy of pines. It was white, seething, inconceivably swift, with a thousand flashing tongues. It traveled ahead of smoke. It was so thin he could see the branches through it, and the fiery clouds behind. It swept onward, a sublime and an appalling spectacle. Sloane could not think of what it looked like. It was fire, liberated, freed from the bowels of the earth, tremendous, devouring.

This, then, was the meaning of fire. This, then, was the horrible fate to befall Lucy.

But no! He thought he must be insane not to be overcome in spirit. Yet he was not. He would beat the flame to Lucy. He felt the loss of something, some kind of a sensation which he ought to have had. Still he rode that race to kill his sweetheart better than any race he had ever before ridden. He kept his seat; he dodged the snags; he pulled the maddened horse the shortest way; he kept the King running straight.

No horse had ever run so magnificent a race! Wildfire was outracing the wind and fire, and he was overhauling the most noted racer of the uplands against a tremendous handicap. But now he was no longer racing to kill the King; he was running in terror. For miles he had held that long, swift, wonderful stride without a break. He was running to his death, whether or not he distanced the fire. Nothing could stop him now but a bursting heart.

Sloane untied his lasso and coiled the noose. Almost within reach of the King! One throw—one sudden swerve—and the King would go down. Lucy would know only a stunning shock. Sloane's heart broke. Could he kill her—crush that dear golden head? He could not, yet he must! He saw a long, curved, red welt on Lucy's white shoulders. What was that? Had a branch lashed her? Sloane could not see her face. She could not have been dead or in a faint, for she was riding the King, bound as she was!

Closer and closer drew Wildfire. He seemed to go faster and faster as that wind of flame gained upon them. The air was too thick to breathe. It had an irresistible weight. It pushed horses and riders onward in their flight—straws on the crest of a cyclone.

Again Sloane looked back, and again the spectacle was different. There was a white and golden fury of flame above, beautiful and blinding; and below, farther back, an inferno of glowing fire, black-streaked, with trembling, exploding puffs and streams of yellow smoke. The aisles between the burning pines were smoky, murky caverns, moving and weird. Sloane saw fire shoot from the treetops down the trunks, and he saw fire shoot up the trunks, like trains of powder. They exploded like huge rockets. And along the forest floor leaped the little flames. His eyes burned and blurred till all merged into a wide, pursuing storm too awful for the gaze of man.

Wildfire was running down the King. The great gray had not lessened his speed, but he was breaking. Sloane felt a ghastly triumph when he began to whirl the noose of the lasso around his head. Already he was within range. But he held back his throw which meant the end of all. And as he hesitated Wildfire suddenly whistled one shrieking blast.

Sloane looked. Ahead there was light through the forest! Sloane saw a white, open space of grass. A park? No! The end of the forest! Wildfire, like a demon, hurtled onward with his smoothness of action gone, beginning to break, within a length of the King.

A cry escaped Sloane—a cry as silent as if there had been no deafening roar, as wild as the race, and as terrible as the ruthless fire. It was the cry of life instead of death. Both the White King and Wildfire would beat the flame.

Then, with the open just ahead Sloane felt a wave of hot wind rolling over him. He saw the lashing tongues of flame above him in the pines. The storm had caught him. It forged ahead. He was riding under a canopy of fire. Burning pine cones, like torches, dropped all around him. He had a terrible blank sense of weight, of suffocation, of the air turning to fire.

Then Wildfire, with his nose at White King's flank, flashed out of the pines into the open. Sloane saw a grassy wide reach inclining gently toward a dark break in the ground with crags rising sheer above it, and to the right a great open space.

Sloane felt that clear air as the breath of deliverance. His reeling sense righted. There the King ran, blindly going to his death. Wildfire was breaking fast. His momentum carried him. He was almost done.

Sloane roped the King, and holding hard, waited for the end. They ran on, breaking, breaking. Sloane thought he would have to throw the King, for they were perilously near the deep cleft in the rim. But the King went to his knees.

Sloane leaped off just as Wildfire fell. How the blade flashed that released Lucy! She was wet from the horse's sweat and foam. She slid off into Sloane's arms, and he called her name. Could she hear above that roar back there in the forest? The pieces of rope hung to her wrists, and Sloane saw dark bruises, raw and bloody. She fell against him. Was she dead? His heart contracted. How white the face! No. He saw her breast heave against his, and he cried aloud, incoherently in his joy. She was alive! She was not badly hurt. She stirred. She plucked at him with nerveless hands. She pressed close to him. He heard her smothered voice, yet so full, so wonderful! . . .

* * * * *

After rejoicing that they were both still alive, belatedly their thoughts turned to their faithful horses. Lucy had long been inseparable from her horse, Wildfire.

How strange that Sloane should run toward the King while Lucy ran to Wildfire!

The King was a beaten, broken horse, but he would live to run another race.

Lucy was kneeling beside Wildfire, sobbing and crying, "Wildfire! Wildfire!"

All of Wildfire was white except where he was red, and that red was not now his glossy, flaming skin. A terrible muscular convulsion, as of internal collapse, grew slower and slower. Yet choked, blinded, dying, killed on his feet, Wildfire heard Lucy's voice.

"Oh, Lin! Oh, Lin!" moaned Lucy.

While they knelt there the violent convulsions changed to slow heaves.

"He ran the King down—carryin' weight—with a long lead to overcome!" Sloane muttered, and he put a shaking hand on the horse's wet neck.

A change, both of body and spirit, seemed to pass over the great stallion.

"Wildfire! Wildfire!"

Again the rider called to his horse, with a low and piercing cry. But Wildfire did not hear.

* * * * *

"Wildfire," by Zane Grey. Reprinted by permission of Loren Grey. Zane Grey (1872–1939) was born in Zanesville, Ohio. He was the highest-selling and highest-paid author in the world during the first half of the twentieth century. He is considered to be the Father of the Western Novel and the last chronicler of the frontier to write while the frontier still existed. He was also one of the leading nature writers of his time.

A Grownup Could Hardly Have Stood It

Lincoln Steffens

For Christmas, the boy wanted not boots, not candy, but just a pony. So when Christmas arrived, but the pony didn't—the boy's heart broke.

* * * * *

What interested me in our new neighborhood was not the school, nor the room I was to have in the house all to myself, but the stable that was built back of the house. My father let me direct the making of a stall, a little smaller than the other stalls, for my pony, and I prayed and hoped. My sister Lou believed that that meant that I would get the pony, perhaps for Christmas. I pointed out to her that there were three other stalls and no horses at all. This I said in order that she should answer it. She could not. My father, when sounded out, said that someday we might have horses and a cow; meanwhile a stable added to the value of the house. "Someday" is a pain to a boy who lives in and knows only "now." My good little sisters, to comfort me, remarked that Christmas was coming, but Christmas was always coming, and grownups were always talking about it, asking you what you wanted and then giving you what they wanted you to have. Though everybody knew what I wanted, I told them all again. My mother knew that I told God, too, every night. I wanted a pony, and to make sure that they understood, I declared that I wanted nothing else.

"Nothing but a pony?" my father asked.

"Nothing," I said.

"Not even a pair of high boots?"

That was hard. I did want boots, but I stuck to the pony. "No, not even boots."

"Nor candy? There ought to be something to fill your stocking with, and Santa Claus can't put a pony into a stocking."

That was true, and he couldn't lead a pony down the chimney, either. But no. "All I want is a pony," I said. "If I can't have a pony, give me nothing, nothing."

Now I had been looking myself for the pony I wanted, going to sales stables, inquiring of horsemen, and I had seen several that would do. My father let me "try" them. I tried so many ponies that I was learning fast to sit a horse. I chose several, but my father always found some fault with them. I was in despair. When Christmas was at hand I had given up all hope of a pony, and on Christmas Eve I hung up my stocking along with my sisters', of whom, by the way, I now had three. I hadn't mentioned them or their coming because, you understand, they were girls, and girls, young girls, counted for nothing in my manly life. They did not mind me either; they were so happy that Christmas Eve that I caught some of their merriment. I speculated on what I'd get; I hung up the biggest stocking I had, and we all went reluctantly to bed to wait till morning. Not to sleep; not right away. We were told that we must not only sleep promptly, we must not wake up till seven-thirty the next morning—or if we did, we must not go to the fireplace for our Christmas presents. Impossible.

We did sleep that night, but we woke up at six o'clock. We lay in our beds and debated through the open doors whether to obey till, say, half-past six. Then we bolted. I don't know who started it, but there was a rush. We all disobeyed; we raced to disobey and get first to the fireplace in the front room downstairs. And there they were, the gifts, all sorts of wonderful things, mixed-up piles of presents; only, as I disentangled the mess, I saw that my stocking was empty; it hung limp; not a thing in it; and under and around it—nothing. My sisters had knelt down, each by her pile of gifts; they were squealing with delight, till they looked up and saw me standing there in my nightgown with nothing. They left their piles to come to me and look with me at my empty place. Nothing. They felt my stocking—nothing.

I don't remember whether I cried at that moment, but my sisters did. They ran with me back to my bed, and there we all cried till I became indignant. That helped some. I got up, dressed, and driving my sisters away, I went alone out into the yard, down to the stable, and there, all by myself, I wept. My mother came out to me by and by; she found me in my pony stall, sobbing on the floor, and she tried to comfort me. But I heard my father outside; he had come part way with her, and she was having some sort of angry quarrel with him. She tried to comfort me; besought me to come to breakfast. I could not. I wanted no comfort and no breakfast. She left me and went on into the house with sharp words for my father.

I don't know what kind of a breakfast the family had. My sisters said it was "awful." They were ashamed to enjoy their own toys. They came to me, and I was rude. I ran away from them. I went around to the front of the house, sat down on the steps, and, the crying over, I ached. I was wronged, I was hurt—I can feel now what I felt then, and I am sure that if one could see the wounds upon our hearts, there would be found still upon mine a scar from that terrible Christmas morning. And my father, the practical joker, he must have been hurt, too, a little. I saw him looking out of the window. He was watching me, or something, for an hour or two, drawing back the curtain ever so little lest I catch him, but I saw his face, and I think I can see now the anxiety upon it, the worried impatience.

After—I don't know how long, surely an hour or two—I was brought to the climax of my agony by the sight of a man riding a pony down the street, a pony and a brand-new saddle; the most beautiful saddle I ever saw, and it was a boy's saddle; the man's feet were not in the stirrups; his legs were too long. The outfit was perfect; it was the realization of all my dreams, the answer to all my prayers. A fine new bridle with a light curb bit. And the pony! As he drew near, I saw that the pony was really a small horse, what we called an Indian pony, a bay, with black mane and tail and one white foot and a white star on his forehead. For such a horse as that I would have given—I could have forgiven—anything.

But the man, a disheveled fellow with a blackened eye and a fresh-cut face, came along, reading the numbers on the houses, and, as my hopes—my impossible hopes—rose, he looked at our door and passed by, he, the pony, the saddle, and the bridle. Too much. I fell upon the steps, and having wept before, I broke now into such a flood of tears that I was a floating wreck when I heard a voice.

"Say, kid," it said, "do you know a boy named Lennie Steffens?"

I looked up. It was the man on the pony, back again at our horse block.

"Yes," I sputtered through my tears. "That's me."

"Well," he said, "then this is your horse. I've been looking all over for you and your house. Why don't you put your number where it can be seen?"

"Get down," I said, running out to him.

He went on saying something about ". . . ought to have got here at seven o'clock; told me to bring the nag here and tie him to your post and leave him for you. But I got into a drunk, and a fight, and a hospital, and—"

"Get down," I said.

He got down, and he boosted me up to the saddle. He offered to fit the stirrups to me, but I didn't want him to. I wanted to ride.

"What's the matter with you?" he said, angrily. "What you crying for? Don't you like the horse? He's a dandy, this horse. I know him of old. He's fine at cattle; he'll drive 'em home."

I hardly heard, I could scarcely wait, but he persisted. He adjusted the stirrups, and then, finally, off I rode, slowly, at a walk, so happy, so thrilled, that I did not know what I was doing. I did not look back at the house or the man; I rode off up the street, taking note of everything—of the reins, of the pony's long mane, of the carved leather saddle. I had never seen anything so beautiful. And mine! I was going to ride up past Miss Kay's house. But I noticed on the horn of the saddle some stains like raindrops, so I turned and trotted home, not to the house, but to the stable. There was the family—father, mother, sisters—all working for me, all happy. They had been putting in place the tools of my new business: blankets, currycomb, brush, pitchfork—everything—and there was hay in the loft.

"What did you come back so soon for?" somebody asked. "Why didn't you go on riding?"

I pointed to the stains. "I wasn't going to get my new saddle rained on," I said.

My father laughed. "It isn't raining," he said. "Those are not raindrops."

"They are tears," my mother gasped, and she gave my father a look that sent him off to the house. Worse still, my mother offered to wipe away the tears still running out of my eyes. I gave her such a look as she had given him, and she went off after my father, drying her own tears. My sisters remained, and we all unsaddled the pony, put on his halter, led him to his stall, tied him, and fed him. It began really to rain; so all the rest of that memorable day we curried and combed that pony. The girls braided his mane, forelock, and tail, while I pitchforked hay to him and curried and brushed, curried and brushed. For a change we brought him out to drink; we led him up and down, blanketed like a race horse; we took turns at that. But the best, the most inexhaustible fun, was to clean him. When we went reluctantly to our midday Christmas dinner, we all smelt of horse, and my sisters had to wash their faces and hands. I was asked to, but I wouldn't, till my mother bade me look in the mirror. Then I washed up—quick. My face was caked with the muddy lines of tears that had coursed over my cheeks to my mouth. Having washed away that shame, I ate my dinner, and as I ate I grew hungrier and hungrier. It was my first meal that day, and as I filled up on the turkey, the stuffing, the cranberries, the pies, the fruit, and the nuts, as I swelled, I could laugh. My mother said I still choked and sobbed now and then, but I laughed, too; I saw and enjoyed my sisters' presents till—I had to go out and attend to my pony, who was there, really and truly there, the promise, the beginning, of a happy double life. And—I went and looked to make sure—there was the saddle, too, and the bridle.

But that Christmas, which my father had planned so carefully, was it the best or the worst that I ever knew? He often asked me that; I never could answer as a boy. I think now that it was both. It covered the whole distance from brokenhearted misery to bursting happiness—too fast. A grownup could hardly have stood it.

* * * * *

"A Grownup Could Hardly Have Stood It," by Lincoln Steffens. Excerpt from The Autobiography of Lincoln Steffens, *copyright © 1931 by Harcourt, Inc., and renewed 1959 by Peter Steffens. Reprinted by permission of Harcourt, Inc. Lincoln Steffens (1866–1936) was not only one of America's most prominent authors at the turn of the nineteenth century, he was also associate editor of* American Magazine *and managing editor of* McClure's Magazine.

CHAMPIONS

Belle Coates

Jon Chapman had been envious of his cousin Grant for a long time. Grant had everything he wanted: the winning team of grays, his lush land—and Arlene Sander, the prettiest girl in the county.

And Jon had . . . a team of scrubs, a hilltop filled with unsightly stumps, a shanty, and plain-looking Melanie Dill.

Finally, Melanie broke through Jon's defeatism with two lines of George Herbert's poetry.

* * * * *

For three years straight, the Chapman grays had won the log-pulling contest at the Fernwoods Harvest Festival. And young Jon Chapman had been proud and wild with joy at their triumph, until this year.

This year Jon watched the gray team win with bitterness in his heart. He and Uncle Tim had raised the handsome, powerful Hugo and Leo from the time they had been colts. He himself had helped feed and groom and train them for this yearly log-pulling event. Silently now he stood back from the side lines, apart from the shouting farmers and woodsmen, while his cousin, Grant Chapman, was presented with the prize, a new set of harness.

Jon watched the triumphant Grant pull off the old harness and buckle on the new with blue ribbons waving at the bridle straps. Then Grant strode toward the group of laughing girls, and Jon held his breath. The owner of the winning team had the right to choose the Queen of the Harvest, and she would be his partner in all the festival events.

Without hesitation Grant Chapman took the hand of Arlene Sander and lifted her lightly to Hugo's broad back, while he swung astride Leo. Jon watched Grant and Arlene ride away together on the winning grays, while the laughing and shouting rose higher and bitterness burned deep within him.

"They won only by a foot," said a small, staunch voice beside Jon.

Jon looked down at Melanie Dill, standing in her blue slacks at his shoulder. "And what of it?" he wanted to know.

The girl nodded toward his shaggy black team, straining restlessly at a hitching post. "You have your colts coming on."

"Those scrubs!" In spite of his bitterness Jon laughed. "Do you imagine that my scrubby blacks could ever win? . . ." He broke off, still more bitter for thinking that Melanie only pitied him, and wanted to comfort him because Grant had the grays.

"They're getting big!" Melanie cried, admiring the blacks. "May I ride Seal as far as my house, Jon?"

"I suppose so." Jon gathered up the old harness that Grant had cast off the grays, dragged it toward his black colts, and tossed it over their necks. Grant had said he could have it. The harness fit the blacks better than he had thought it would. The scrubs *were* getting bigger, but they were still scrubs and always would be. They couldn't pull.

"I always get the leavings," he burst out, as he and Melanie rode out of town. "The old harness, the scrub team, the poorest patch of land."

The plainest girl, thought Melanie ruefully to herself. Melanie Dill knew that Jon had wanted to ride home with Arlene. Arlene was the prettiest girl in the Fernwoods country.

Since their uncle's retirement and departure to California the winter before, Jon and Grant Chapman had been on their own. In the division of the property, Grant, the older cousin, had been given the hay meadow and the team of champion grays. Jon fell heir to the scrub colts, the woods and stump land, and the old cabin in the timber.

Jon liked working with wood better than with crops; his uncle had known that. But it was their uncle's favoring Grant in the division of the horses that hurt, Jon admitted to himself. Grant didn't understand the handling of the grays, had no use for the heavy team in gardening and hay making, while he, Jon, could use them to good advantage in hauling out timber. The black colts would not pull together, were skittish and clumsy. They dodged through open gates and were hard to catch.

"Your Uncle Tim knows that ever since you played with marbles and tricycles, you've always thought what Grant had was best," Melanie reminded Jon with sisterly frankness as she slipped off Seal's back at her own gate. "So maybe he took you up on it this time, just to see if you'd do something about it."

Jon looked at her, puzzled, and she added, giving him her warm smile in parting, "Once I made a quilt out of some silk leavings, and it won first prize at the fair."

* * * * *

One morning in November, Jon saw Melanie coming through his timber with a neat brown hen tucked under her arm and a determined glint in her brown eyes.

"What's that for?" he demanded, as she placed the hen beside the log where he sat restlessly gnawing a twig. "To stew in that copper kettle you gave me last week?"

"That hen," Melanie explained sternly, "is to put in your chicken house—if you own such a building—to lay some eggs and start you a flock. It's high time," she added, as the hen scratched busily among the litter in Jon's neglected dooryard, "that someone started to scratch around here."

Jon grinned sheepishly. "Meaning that I'm lazy?"

"Worse," she corrected soberly. "You're envious. Move over, Jon, and let me sit down. Ever hear this couplet by George Herbert?

"Envy not greatness: for thou mak'st thereby
Thyself the worse, and so the distance greater."

"Worse, and so the distance greater," Jon repeated, with his moody eyes upon Grant's champion grays in the meadow below. "The distance between my blacks and Grant's grays is so great that—"

Melanie interrupted, "You envy Grant everything—his horses, his house, his land, his girl. That's not healthy, Jon. It's making you aloof, moody, and defeated. No wonder Arlene likes Grant best. Why don't you try earning for yourself some of the things that you envy in Grant? Make use of what you have and—"

"And what do I have but hills and stumps?"

"You have the finest stand of timber in all of Fernwood country, the prettiest home site on this knoll. You have two strong arms, a good-enough team. Pull out all these hideous stumps, turn your cabin into a chicken house, and build yourself a good log house. You have poles and logs galore."

"What a high-powered advisor you've turned out to be," mocked Jon. But the next morning he hitched the black colts to the stump puller and went at the stumps on the knoll.

* * * * *

By spring Jon had the knoll cleared of the unsightly stumps and the foundation started to his rustic log house. During the long winter evenings, he and Melanie had pored over the plans to the new log house, the best wall for the fireplace, the height of the sink. There came a month of bitter, freezing weather that halted the building, but Jon drove the blacks into the timber and hauled more logs, trimmed poles. His restlessness had become a prod, goading him toward the goal of fulfillment. The month of June saw the house up, and a new pole fence around the whole place.

One day, he drove the blacks, Seal and Serge, down the hill to try to pull the old oak stump. The blacks had not yet been able to move it. It was the toughest stump, the last one left to mar the sweep of his hillside.

He whistled as he fastened the cable around the oak stump. He had spent months of work, turning his foolish wishing into an urge, a driving force to accomplish and win, and now he felt happier. Melanie had been right. His log house suited him even better than Grant's, which needed paint badly. His hilly stump land, with the fine stand of timber behind it, would soon be as clean and pretty as the floor of Grant's meadow. Wait until Arlene saw it!

That afternoon, while Melanie watched from her perch on the new pole fence, the blacks pulled out the oak stump.

"The colts are steadying down, Jon. They can pull."

"They're doing all right," Jon admitted, running his hand over Seal's powerful black shoulder, rubbing Serge's soft nose. "For scrubs," he added. But what a time he had had with them at first, as they caught their clumsy

feet in the stump puller, wanting to gallop with a load of logs, jerking unevenly at every pull he set them to.

"They're almost as big as Grant's grays now," Melanie praised.

Jon glanced down the hill toward Grant's meadow, where Hugo and Leo stood dozing while Grant was in the city.

"Grant's not taking the right care of them," said Melanie. "They've stood idle all summer. And he drove them on too many sleighing parties last winter. The grays are too heavy for that. It spoils them," she said.

Late in August, Grant harnessed the Chapman grays and drove them through Jon's gate, hailing him boisterously, "Howdy, stump farmer! Mind if I take Hugo and Leo up in your timber to practice a little log-pulling before the big event?"

"Go ahead," Jon consented, turning to wave Seal and Serge back from the barnyard gate that Grant had left open in passing through.

Grant glanced briefly at the colts and laughed. "The scrubs are still up to their old tricks dodging through gates, aren't they, Jon?"

One evening a week later, after Grant drove the perspiring grays home, Jon walked up into his timber. He could see where Grant had hitched the grays, first to small logs, then to medium-sized ones, and finally to the largest oak log, which was the size of the one usually used in the log-pulling contest. He saw where their great straining hoofs had scored the earth, but he could not tell if they had moved it.

"Why don't you see if Seal and Serge can move it?" suggested Melanie, coming up with a pail of berries.

Jon laughed shortly, knowing well the thought back of her question. The Harvest Festival, with the log-pulling contest as the first event, was only two weeks away.

"No, Melanie, that's out," he refused defiantly. "I'm not foolish enough to imagine that my scrubs would have any chance against Grant's champs, even if the champs are a little out of training. So forget it."

Melanie sighed.

* * * * *

With his stumps out, his house and fence completed, Jon had begun getting in his winter's wood, snaking the heavy logs through the timber to his dooryard, ready for final sawing and chopping. On the day before the log-pulling contest he found that Grant's grays, in their practice, had pulled the oak log across the road, blocking his way with the wood.

He unhitched Seal and Serge from their load, hitched them to the oak log, and swung it out of his way.

"Bravo!" called a delighted girlish voice.

Jon wheeled to see Arlene Sander coming through the woods with her arms full of yellow leaves.

"So this is why I haven't seen you since I got back," she chided. "You're busy training another champion team for the Harvest Festival."

"My blacks are scrubs, not champions," Jon corrected, noticing that her fair hair was the same gold as the leaves. "Besides, I'm not training them. This log—"

"Champions," Arlene insisted imperiously, placing her slim hand on Seal's nose. "Grant told me last night that his grays could barely move that log. Your blacks swung it around as if it had been a feather."

With a new confidence singing in his heart, Jon showed Arlene his log house, surrounded by scratching brown hens and pink geraniums. He knew what he would do now. He would win tomorrow's log-rolling contest with his team of blacks. Arlene's artless praise of them held a weight that Melanie's staunch loyalty never had.

It was dark that night, and Jon was in bed when he heard Grant drive his grays through his barnyard after their last practice with the log. Grant was worried. Jon wondered if Arlene had mentioned that Jon's blacks had moved the log and were going to compete with the grays in tomorrow's contest.

Jon felt a little sorry for Grant, whom he had formerly envied. Grant had not kept his champions up to their mark, so that now a scrub team of blacks was going to defeat them. Jon slept, dreaming of Arlene riding on Seal's powerful back.

* * * * *

Melanie was right. The blacks were ready to win. Working with wood, big wood, was their business. They had pulled stumps and hauled logs and poles until the barrels of their bodies, their deep chests, were filled with a great stored-up tireless strength. Scrubs or champions, that was enough. Jon had made the most of what he had, and the champions had taken care of themselves.

Jon Chapman's blacks were hitched in their turn to the great log, and with Jon at the reins they moved it. They pulled the great log twice as far as any other team, steadily, easily.

The crowd of farmers and woodsmen broke into a deafening roar of applause. With his hands trembling with joy Jon Chapman accepted the prize harness with the blue ribbons streaming from the bridle straps. Proudly he strapped it about his black champions. Then he turned toward the group of girls from whom it was now his privilege to choose the Harvest Queen.

From the center of the group Arlene Sander smiled prettily, waiting to be chosen. But now that he owned the champions, Jon Chapman knew that Arlene, whose admiration seemed to change as champions changed, did not belong on a champion's back. His eyes swept past her, sought another girl, a brown-eyed girl in blue slacks, who had shown him the futility of envy, giving her hens and her help, scolding, praising, until he had learned that champions, as well as prize quilts, can be made from leavings.

With a happy smile Jon took Melanie Dill's warm hand and swung her triumphantly to her place on Seal's back.

* * * * *

"Champions," by Belle Coates. Published January 30, 1938, in Young People's Weekly. *Reprinted by permission of Joe Wheeler (P.O. Box 1246, Conifer, Colorado 80433) and Cook Communication Ministries, Colorado Springs, Colorado. Belle Coates wrote for inspirational and popular magazines during the first half of the twentieth century.*

Our Horse of a Different Color

Penny Porter

Its father was a white stud with chestnut spots and a multicolored tail that touched the ground, and its mother was covered with thousands of copper dots. So this appaloosa would outshine them both; it would be named Starburst.

That was what was supposed *to happen. Instead . . .*

* * * * *

"When it comes to horses, what you want and what you get are often two different things." Bill, weary from building a new hay barn, kept up his warning to me even as he fell asleep that night.

But I am a dreamer, and foaling season is a time for dreams. After years of raising Hereford cattle on our Arizona ranch, we'd just become appaloosa breeders, and I was dreaming of precious foals, blue ribbons, and eager buyers.

That first year, the dazzling hair-coats of nine little appaloosas had already transformed our pastures into a landscape of color. Their tiny faces were bright with stars and blazes, their rumps glittering with patches and spots splashed over them like suds.

Bill and I were sure our tenth foal of the year, due before dawn, would be the most colorful of all. Its father was a white stud with chestnut spots over more than half his body and a multicolored tail that touched the ground. The mother was covered with thousands of penny-sized copper dots. I already had a name for their unborn treasure: Starburst.

Normally, I would have been awaiting this new arrival in our freezing corral, numb fingers clutching a flashlight. But tonight was different. Bill had bought me a closed-circuit TV, which he set up on my side of the bed. That way, I could watch the monitor in comfort and observe the mare's progress. Then when she reached her last stage of labor, if help was needed, I'd rush to her side.

Now, on the screen, I could see the spotted mare's hide glistening with sweat. White-rimmed eyes betrayed her anxiety, and dust devils swirled like headless ghosts in the wake of her pacing hooves. Suddenly she stopped cold. Nostrils wide, ears twitching back and forth, she listened for dangers in the night. *It'll be a while yet until she foals,* I thought, and I dozed off.

I awoke with a jolt. Three hours had passed. A glance at the monitor revealed the mare stretched out flat out on her side, steam rising from her body in the frosty air. The birth was over. But where was her foal? I sat up fast, studying the screen and searching the fuzzy shadows and distant corners of the corral. It was gone!

"Bill! Wake up!" I shook him hard. "Something stole the baby!"

Wild dogs, hungry coyotes, and bobcats raided my imagination. I was the one who walked the night when we had calves or foals being born, and I remembered catching a raccoon slaughtering my chickens in the moonlight. I remembered a bobcat, daggers glinting from his eyes, as he slithered across the roof of our rabbit hutch. One midnight, I'd even seen a bear lumbering past our mailbox.

Moments later, after leaping into my jeans and sneakers and grabbing a jacket, I was on my knees in the dimly lit corral, stroking the mare's neck. "Where's your baby, Mama?" I called, almost crying in panic. "Where'd it go?"

Suddenly a plaintive whinny rose from behind the water trough. Then I saw a face pop out of the shadows—thin, long, dark, and ugly. The ears hung like charred pot holders from a rusty hook. Right away, I realized why I hadn't seen this newborn on my TV. No colorful spots. No blazing coat. The foal was brown as dirt.

"I don't believe it," I said, as Bill crouched down beside me for a closer look. "There's not a single white hair on her." We saw more unwanted

traits: a bulging forehead, a hideous, sloping Roman nose, and a nearly hairless bobtail.

"She's a real throwback," Bill said, standing up. I knew we were both thinking the same thing. This filly would be just another mouth to feed. She'd never sell. After all, who wants an appaloosa without color?

By now the spotted mare was on her feet, eyeing this trembling little stranger with contempt. The foal staggered toward her and tried to nurse. The mare wheeled and kicked, knocking the baby to the ground in a scrambled heap. It cried out with fear and surprise.

"Whoa, Mama!" Bill shouted. "Stop that!" He lifted the foal back on her feet. "I'll get the mare some hay," he said. "She needs to be by herself." I knew he was right. Nature would take care of bonding if we left them alone. But after Bill tossed some alfalfa on the ground, hoping to quiet the mare, the filly tried to nurse again. This time the kick was so violent it sent the baby skidding under the fence.

"Oh, Bill," I pleaded, wrapping my arms around the shivering foal, "help me stand her up—just one more time." Once she was on her feet, I stayed with her a minute, steadying her. "You'll be OK, little one," I murmured. "Just keep on trying." I hated to leave, but knew it was best.

The next morning, when Scott arrived for work and saw our newest addition, he minced no words. "What are we going to do with that ugly thing?" he asked.

By now, the baby had nursed, but it looked like all the nourishment had gone to her ears. They stood straight up in the air. "She looks just like a mule," Scott said. "Who's going to want her?"

Our younger girls, Becky and Jaymee, fifteen and twelve, had questions of their own. "How will anyone know she's an appaloosa?" Becky asked. "Are there spots under the fur?"

"No," I told her, "she's what's called a 'solid.' That means no breed characteristics at all. But she's still an appy inside."

That's when Jaymee came up with the glorious wisdom of a twelve-year-old. "That means she's got spots on her heart."

Who knows, I wondered. *Maybe she does.*

From the beginning, the homely filly seemed to sense she was different. Visitors rarely looked at her, for which we were glad. We didn't want to bring attention to the fact that our beautiful stallion had sired this ugly foal. After all, mare owners seeking an appaloosa stud want to be convinced he produces only quality babies with small heads, straight legs, neat little ears, long flowing tails, and—above all—a coat of many colors.

When the filly was two weeks old, we turned her and her mother out to pasture with the herd. Being the newcomer, she was afraid to romp with the other foals because their mothers bared their teeth at her. Worse still, her own mother now seemed to sense her offspring needed all the protection she could get. So she angrily charged any horse that came within fifteen feet of her little one. Even if another foal ventured too close, the mother lashed out with a vicious snap. Little by little, our bobtailed filly learned the world was a place to fear.

Before long, I started noticing something else—she relished human company. She and her mother were first at the gate at feeding time and, when I scratched her neck and shoulder, her eyelids closed in contentment. Soon she was nuzzling my jacket, running her lips over my shirt, chewing my buttons, and even opening the gate to follow me so she could rub her head on my hip.

"Mom's got herself another lame duck," I overheard Scott say to his dad one day.

Bill sighed. "Oh, no, what is it this time?"

"That jugheaded filly. What else?"

Unfortunately, her appetite was huge. And the bigger she got, the uglier she got. *Where will we ever find a home for her?* I wondered.

One day a man bought a beautiful two-year-old "leopard" gelding from us for a circus. He spied the brown bobtailed filly. "That's not an appaloosa, is it?" he asked. "Looks like a donkey."

Since he was looking for circus horses, I snatched at the opportunity. "You'd be surprised," I said. "That filly knows more tricks than a short-order cook. She can take a handkerchief out of my pocket and Rolaids out of Bill's. She can crawl under fences, climb into water troughs, turn on spigots."

"Reg'lar little devil, huh?" he said.

"No, not really. As a matter of fact, I named her Angel!"

He chuckled. "Well, it's eye-catchin' color we need at the Big Top," he told me. "Folks like spotted horses best."

I knew he was right, but as his truck and trailer rattled down the dirt road, I pictured our homely filly jumping through flaming hoops with white poodles in pink tutus clinging to her back. Why couldn't a plain brown horse do the same thing? I wondered.

As time passed, Angel, as we now called her, invented new tricks. Her favorite was opening gates to get food on the opposite side. "She's a regular Houdini," Bill marveled.

"She's a regular pain," said Scott, who always had to catch her.

"Maybe two chains and double clips will work better than one," I suggested. It made no difference. Angel's hunger for anything edible on the other side of the fence persisted, and the jingle-jangle of horse teeth against metal chains on corral gates never stopped as she honed her skills.

With Angel's huge appetite, I tried giving her an extra flake of hay before bed. Her affection for me grew. Unfortunately, so did her appetite. One morning Scott found her in the hay barn, whinnying a greeting. Broken bales littered the floor. Her sides bulged. Scott was disgusted.

"You've got to be more patient and give her some attention, Scott," I told him. "You spend all your time grooming and training the other yearlings. You never touch Angel except to yell at her."

"Who has time to work with a jughead?" he grumbled. "Besides, Dad said we're taking her to auction."

"What! And sell her for dog food?"

I corralled Bill. "Let her grow up on the ranch," I begged. "Then Scott can saddle-break her when she's two. With her sweet nature she'll be worth something to someone by then."

"I guess one more horse won't hurt for the time being," he said. "We'll put her down on the east pasture. There's not much grazing there, but . . ." He was keeping his options open. Still, Angel was safe—for now.

Two weeks later she was at the front door eating dry dog food from our dog's bowl. She'd slipped the chain off the pasture gate and let herself out—plus ten other horses as well. By the time Scott and Bill had rounded them up, I could see that Bill's patience was wearing thin. He turned to the girls. "You two, give her some attention. School's out now. Maybe you can even make her pretty."

That summer, they groomed her, bathed her—and looked for spots. They even rubbed mayonnaise and Swedish hair-grow into the stubbly mane and tail. This folk remedy worked with some horses, but not with Angel. When they tried to brush her teeth, she simply ate the toothbrush. That was on top of all the cantaloupes and watermelons they fed her. She ate everything. Angel loved all the attention, and, perhaps to show it, she even stopped opening gates.

Then school started, and Angel lost her playmates. Scott came into the kitchen one morning, fuming. "That filly's gotta go, Mom," he said. "She got into the tack room last night, pulled bridles off the hooks, knocked saddles on the floor, chewed up a tube of toothpaste the girls left on the sink. She's gonna stay in that east pasture if we have to build a wall around it."

Fortunately, the rain came. The grass grew. Angel stayed in without a wall, and now she got fat as a buffalo—and her assortment of tricks grew. When Bill or Scott drove to the field to check on the herd, she'd chew the side mirrors off the truck, eat the rubber off the windshield wipers, or bend the aerial. If they left a window open, she'd poke her head inside, snatch a rag, wrench, glove, or notebook off the front seat and run away with it.

Surprisingly, Bill began forgiving Angel's pranks. In fact, soon we found ourselves looking forward to her best stunt of all. When an appaloosa buyer would arrive, Angel would come at a gallop, slide to a stop about thirty feet away and back up to have her rump scratched. "We have our own circus right here," Bill told buyers. By now, a small smile was even showing through Scott's thick mustache.

The seasons rolled by. Scorching sun brought rain—and flies by the millions. One day, when Angel was two-and-a-half, I saw Scott leading her to the barn. Her rump was raw, bleeding, and crawling with maggots from the hopeless thwacking of her hairless bobtail. "She gets no protection at all from that stupid tail," Scott told me as he treated Angel with antibiotics. "I'm gonna make her a new one." That's when I realized Scott's feelings for the horse were starting to change.

I smiled as he cut and twisted two dozen strands of bright yellow baling twine into a long string mop and fastened it with adhesive wrap around her bandaged tail. "There," he patted her and stepped back to admire his handiwork, "she looks almost like a normal horse."

When Angel recovered, Scott decided to break her for riding. Bill and I sat on the corral fence as he put on the saddle. Angel humped her back. "We're going to have a rodeo here!" I whispered. But as Scott tightened the cinch around her plump middle, she didn't try to lie down and roll on the ground as some young horses do. She simply waited. When he climbed aboard and applied gentle pressure with his knees, the willing heart of the appaloosa showed. He ordered her forward, and she responded as though she'd been ridden for years.

I reached up and scratched her bulging forehead. "Some day she's going to make a terrific trail-riding horse," I said, taking a moment to admire her tail. Every new shipment of baling twine came in different colors, red, orange, yellow, black. Today her tail was blue.

Scott seemed to know what I was thinking. "Blue's for winners, Mom," he said. "With a temperament like this, someone could even play polo off her. Or she could be a great kid's horse."

Now, even Scott was having a few dreams of his own for our plain brown appaloosa with the funny colored tail.

Angel was soon helping Scott train young foals. Riding her, Scott would clip one end of a rope to a yearling's halter and wrap the other end around the saddle horn. Angel would then pull, even drag, the younger horse along, but always with care.

At foaling time, she whinnied to the newborns as though each one were her own. "We ought to breed her," I said to Bill. "She's four. With her capacity to love, imagine what a good mother she'd make."

"Hey, that's not such a bad idea. People often buy bred mares," he said. "Maybe we'd find a home for her." Suddenly I saw Scott frowning. *Could he really care?* I wondered.

For the first nine months of Angel's pregnancy, Scott kept her busy exercising yearlings. For once, she seemed to forget about escaping from her corral. Also, winter offered only dry, parched fields so the temptation to get out was gone until a heavy rain came and our fields burst to life. She was getting closer to her due date, and I tried not to hear the jingle of a chain because in my heart I knew Angel would once more start slipping through the gates in quest of greener pastures.

One morning we awoke to an unseasonable cold snap. I was starting breakfast when Scott opened the kitchen door, his hazel eyes looming dark beneath the broad-brimmed Stetson. "It's Angel, Mom," he said. "You'd better come. She got out of the corral last night."

Trying to hold back my fears, I followed him to his pickup. "She's had her foal somewhere," he said, "but Dad and I couldn't find it. She's . . . dying." I could hear the catch in his throat. He never got this close to animals. "Ate too much new grass or maybe a poisonous weed." Suddenly his voice broke. "She's halfway between my house and here. Looks like she was trying . . . to make it home."

I scarcely heard him as unbidden memories rolled through my mind—the jingling of a security clasp, the rattle of chain, the creak of an old wooden gate being swung open. And now, last night, silhouetted against the rising moon, nostrils wide, testing secrets in the wind, our horse that nobody wanted had escaped for the last time.

When we got to Angel, Bill was crouched beside her, his boots sinking into the mud. "There's nothing we can do," he said, nodding toward the lush green fields, an easy reach for a hungry horse through the barbed wire. "Too much fresh alfalfa can be a killer."

I pulled Angel's huge head onto my lap and stroked the worn softness that the halter had left behind her too-big ears—those same ears that had made me think of charred pot holders when I had found our dirt-brown filly hidden behind the water trough four years before.

Tears welled in Scott's eyes as he knelt beside me. "Best mare we ever had, Mom," he murmured.

"Angel," I pleaded, "please don't go!" But I felt our mare with all those "spots on her heart" slipping away. Choking back my grief, I ran my hand down the gentle darkness of her beautiful warm brown fur and listened to the heavy, labored breathing. The long legs strained, and her neck arched desperately backward, seeking one last breath of air. She shuddered. I looked into eyes that could no longer see. Angel was gone.

Then in a cloud of numbness I heard Scott call out only a few yards away, disbelief in his voice. "Mom . . . Mom! Here's the foal. I found the foal!"

Deep in the sweet-smelling grasses where Angel had hidden him lay the foal of our dreams. A single spot brightened his tiny face, and a scattering of stars spangled his back and hips. A pure, radiant appaloosa. Our horse of many colors. "Starburst," I whispered.

But somehow, all that color didn't matter any more. As his mother had taught us so many times over: It's not what's on the outside that counts; it's what lies deep in the heart. That's where Angel's spots and beauty were. It's that way with all animals—and it's that way with people too.

* * * * *

"Our Horse of a Different Color," by Penny Porter. Published September 1995 in Reader's Digest *and in Porter's anthology,* Heartstrings and Tail-Tuggers *(Ravenhawk Books, 1999). Reprinted by permission of the author.* Reader's Digest *has published more of Penny Porter's true-life animal stories than those of any other author. Today, she lives and writes from her home in Tucson, Arizona.*

How Old Major Preached a Sermon

Sara Virginia Dubois

Since the weather was getting worse by the minute, it was decided that they'd stay home from church and spare their poor horse.

But someone forgot to tell Old Major.

* * * * *

A cold, northeast storm swept against the kitchen window, and Mr. Leeds went to the door to inspect the weather.

"Terribly bad weather, this," he said. "It would hardly be merciful to take Old Major out this morning. I calculate we would better stay at home from service today."

Mrs. Leeds stopped in her preparations and looked thoughtfully at her husband. "We are not in the habit of staying at home on account of the weather," she said. "Still, if it seems the proper thing to do, I have nothing to say."

James came running in from the barn, banging the door after him. "It is getting worse all the time, Father," he said, "but Old Major is roughshod. I don't think it will hurt him. And we can take plenty of blankets along to keep us dry."

"We will spend the day at home, James," Mr. Leeds said. "It hardly seems fair to Old Major to take him out in such weather. It might not do us any harm, but a righteous man considers the life of his beasts."

"I suppose there will not be many out," said Mrs. Leeds, as she seated herself with open Bible. "Grandfather Strouber may drop in, but he has only to step out of his back door into the side entrance of the church. And the good old soul can't hear a word after he gets there, not even the singing. But his daughter-in-law says he receives his share of the blessing."

The morning slipped quietly by, and Mr. Leeds sat poring over a recent copy of the church paper. James had an issue of the young people's paper, and Mrs. Leeds was diligently studying the Sabbath School lesson. When the clock struck one, Mrs. Leeds began making preparations for dinner.

"I'll run out and feed Old Major," said James. "It is not storming now as it was an hour or so ago."

"Give him plenty of oats," said Mr. Leeds, kindly. "He always has a heaping measure on Sabbath."

"Father," cried James a few moments later, bounding into the kitchen and leaving the door wide open. "Old Major has slipped his halter, and I cannot find him anywhere."

"Here he comes down the road," cried Mrs. Leeds, excitedly. "I do believe he has been to church after all."

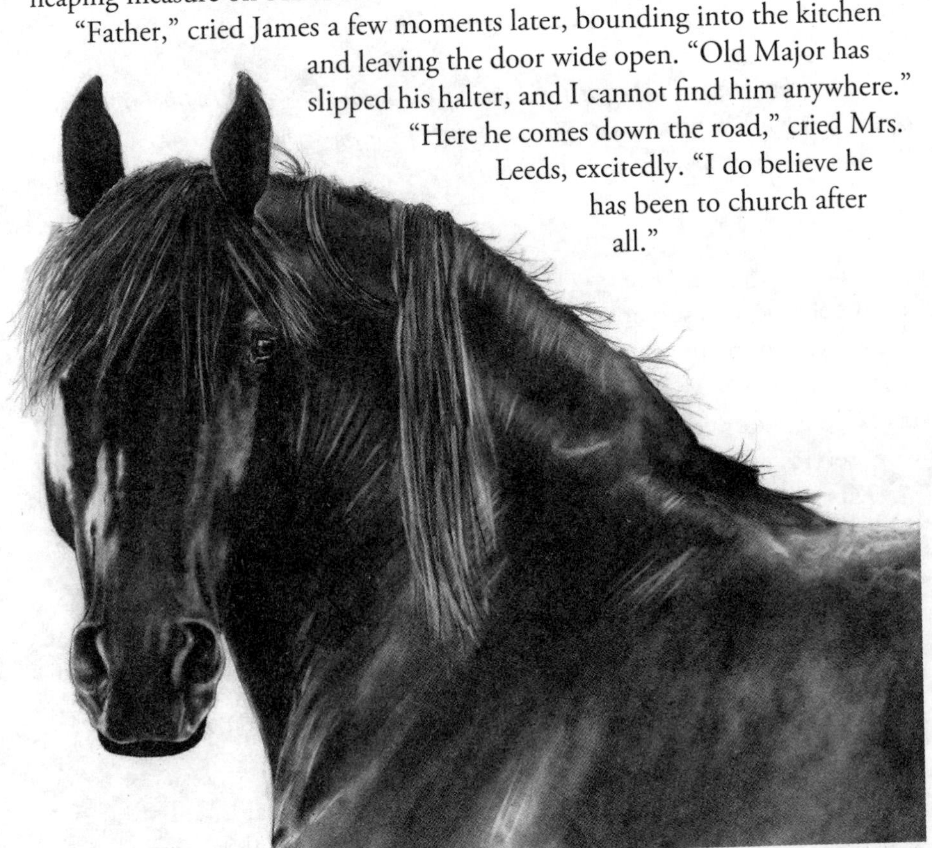

Sure enough, just as the minister entered the churchyard, Old Major had walked up the drive and sought the shed where he was sheltered every Sabbath.

"Well, I never!" said Mrs. Leeds, as she lifted the boiling kettle from the fire. "If old Major hasn't given us a sermon, then I am mistaken."

Mr. Leeds looked over his shoulder in her direction and smiled. "The most forceful sermon I ever heard in my life. We are not going to mind the weather next time, are we?"

* * * * *

"How Old Major Preached a Sermon," by Sara Virginia Dubois. Published January 28, 1919, in The Youth's Instructor. *Reprinted by permission of Joe Wheeler (P.O. Box 1246, Conifer, Colorado 80433) and Review and Herald® Publishing Association, Hagerstown, Maryland. Sara Virginia Dubois wrote for inspirational magazines during the first half of the twentieth century.*

Illustration on page 40 used by permission of the artist, Ashley Applegate.

The Ride of Deborah Lee

Chandler Briggs Allen

The War of 1812 was raging. Once again, America was at war with England. Deborah Lee's most precious possession was her spirited horse, Bonnie Dell, and the British were going to steal the horse from her.

What should she do?

* * * * *

Deborah Lee stood in the doorway of the roomy, weather-beaten house nestling under a wide-spreading elm halfway up the hill that inclined gently upward from the river to the tree line above. The pine-crowned tops of the distant eastern hills shone like burnished gold in the last lingering rays of the September sun, but the shades of early twilight were creeping over river and valley. The leaves of the lofty elm rustled softly in the evening breeze, and the low, sighing song of the pines on the upland came in a faint whisper to her ears.

But the golden glory of the hills was unseen and the evening song of the trees unheard by the girl in the doorway. The air seemed to be surcharged with a vague forewarning of impending danger as she gazed with anxious eyes at the three black hulks out on the darkening river. From the village below came the intermittent murmur of voices and an occasional bark of a dog or a loud-voiced exclamation. The clatter of dishes and tinkle of tin told of one housewife who refused to neglect her after-supper duties, but no sound of laughter came to Deborah Lee. She knew, as did the other good people of Frankfort, that the *Dragon,* the *Sylph*, and the *Perunion*, ships of the British Navy, swung at anchor on the broad Penobscot and that the troops crowded on and between decks would be landed early next morning. There were rumors that a party of soldiers would land and take possession of the town that night, and Deborah's breath came a little faster, and the pink faded from her cheeks as she saw three dark objects moving across the water and the measured sound of oars came to her listening ears. The rumor had proved to be true. The British were landing that evening.

It was the first day of September 1814. Early that morning the sound of great guns had been heard far to the south. At noon a courier had galloped into the village bringing tidings of the fall of Castine. Later in the day another messenger had arrived on a foam-flecked, exhausted horse with the news that General Gosselin had crossed the river with two ships and six hundred men to occupy Belfast.

Then, just as the sun sank below the western hills, three vessels flying the British flag had dropped anchor before the village, and the danger that had seemed far-off and vague became very real and near. No one had expected the British to visit the village, and their arrival filled all with alarm. No one ventured to foretell just what the troops would do when they landed, but the general belief was that something terrible would take place. People were hiding their money and valuables in safe places or burying them in the ground. Job Winslow passed by, leading a horse. He saw Deborah and shouted, "You'd better get Bonny Dell out o' sight or them Britishers will steal her!"

Steal Bonny Dell! Steal her own snow-white horse that her uncle had brought from the south five years before when Bonny Dell was a little colt! She had not thought that anyone could be so wicked as even to think of such a thing. Startled and alarmed, she turned and ran into the house. How lonely and empty it seemed. Her father and brother had gone that afternoon to join the force at Hampden, where General Blake was preparing for battle, leaving Deborah with Nancy Holmes, who, since the death of Deborah's mother seven years before, had acted as housekeeper at the Lee home.

Nancy, reading her Bible by the light of a tallow candle, looked up as

Deborah rushed in, crying, "Oh, Nancy! The British are landing, and Mr. Winslow says they will steal Bonny Dell! What shall I do?"

Nancy Holmes closed the Book she loved. Deborah was very dear to the lonely old lady. She smiled affectionately, and her brave old voice was vibrant with encouragement as she replied; *"Do?* Why, don't let them steal her! Take Bonny Dell over to the old house in the woods. They'll never find her there! The British aren't goin' to stay on the Penobscot long, deary."

"But, Nancy, the British will go up to Hampden, and there'll be a battle, and Father and Brother Henry and . . . and . . . William. . . ." The tears were falling now, and Deborah's voice quivered.

"I know, Deb. I know how you feel, dear; but the same Lord that gave us all strength and faith in the Revolution is living today, and He'll protect us now just as He did then. I know what it is to worry, Deb. Paul Holmes and I were only a month married when he enlisted, and for six years there was hardly a day that I didn't wonder whether I was a wife or a widow. You know the road to Hampden, Deb. Why not take Bonny Dell and go? I shall be safe here. No one will harm an old woman like me."

"I'm not afraid of them!" Deborah's voice was strong again, and the color had returned to her cheeks. "I'll take Bonny Dell to the old house, and I'll stay here. I have a right to be in my father's house; the British shall not drive me away!"

Bonny Dell greeted her mistress with a whinny, but Deborah was in too much haste to give her the caresses she expected. The homely old side-saddle was thrown on and the bridle adjusted in a manner that surprised the white horse. A minute sufficed for Deborah to fill a bag with oats, throw it on behind the saddle, and spring on the horse's back.

Bonny Dell was a magnificent creature. Arabian blood ran in her veins. Her coat of pure white, her long mane and heavy tail were creamy in color. Deep of chest and clean-limbed, she possessed remarkable intelligence, wonderful endurance, and speed.

No wonder that Bonny Dell would be coveted by any British officer who should catch sight of her. Such a horse would be a magnificent prize and, if seen, would surely be taken by the invaders.

The mile to the deserted house in the woods was quickly covered, and Bonny Dell, secreted from prying eyes, with a supply of oats before her, was safe for the night.

Deborah walked home through the dark woods to find that visitors had arrived during her absence. They were unwelcome guests, too, for they were British officers.

Both arose as she entered and bowed courteously. Deborah concealed her surprise and embarrassment as she acknowledged their salutation in the formal manner of that time and then retired, saying she must help Nancy prepare supper for them.

The older officer resumed his seat, but Lieutenant Bruce stood looking at the door behind which Deborah had vanished.

" 'Tis a happy fortune that brought us here, Captain Meiklejohn," he remarked at length in a low tone, turning to his superior.

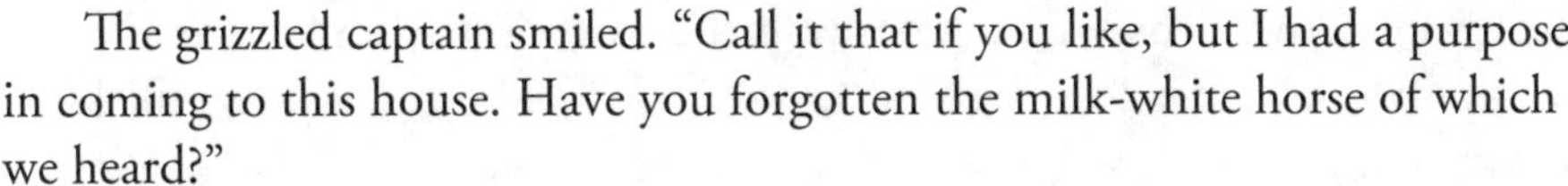

The grizzled captain smiled. "Call it that if you like, but I had a purpose in coming to this house. Have you forgotten the milk-white horse of which we heard?"

"Ay, I recall the gossip of the old woman and her hang-dog son. Do you mean . . . ?" He hesitated and looked toward the half-open door.

The captain laughed silently. " 'Tis yon lass who owns the nag," he said in a half-whisper.

"Surely, you would not take her horse!"

Deborah, in the kitchen, heard the lieutenant's exclamation, and the pewter platter of ham and eggs nearly dropped from her hands as she started in alarm. Her heart almost stopped its beating as she listened to the answer.

"And why should I not? 'Tis a lawful prize of war to the army."

"Nay, Captain, trouble her not. Horses there are in plenty, but maids like this one are rare!"

"Trouble or no trouble," came the growling response, "I'll see the brute in the morning and take it if it suits me. I'll give the girl a five-pound note if I take her horse. These Yankees care for nothing but money, I am told. And now," his tone changed, "are the roads guarded? We want no telltale clodhopper sneaking through with information."

Deborah controlled herself and stood listening, as motionless as a marble statue. Every word spoken in the next room came to her distinctly.

"The men are stationed as you ordered, sir. Every road is guarded and men watch every bypath and woods road that the youth told us of." The lieutenant's voice was cold, and Deborah, inclining her head a little, could see him standing erect with arms folded. She had recognized the woman and son of whom he had spoken, and her cheeks burned with indignation as she thought of their treachery.

She forced herself to assist in preparing the table and when, a few minutes later, she summoned the officers to their supper, no trace of emotion lingered on her face.

She replied civilly to the captain's remarks and smiled pleasantly when the lieutenant spoke to her, but left the room after their wants had been supplied.

Ham and eggs, hot cornbread and potatoes, with jelly of Nancy's own making kept the hungry officers quiet for a while.

"Small wonder that roses bloom in her cheeks!" laughed the young lieutenant. "Such wholesome food washed down with rich milk would tinge with pink even the faded cheeks of Lady Coldbrook! But why stays the lass away?"

"Mayhap she sees not the charms in you that you have discovered in her," the captain suggested. "We wear the colors of our king—God bless him—and to her, we are enemies. And now for the plans of tomorrow."

Deborah, listening intently in the next room as they talked, could hear the plans of the impending attack.

For a half hour they sat and discussed the situation, but at last the arrival of a sergeant interrupted the conference. All was well, the sergeant informed them, and with this assurance the officers were shown to their rooms by Nancy and retired.

Deborah lay awake a long time thinking of what she had heard. Already she had thought of a plan to save Bonny Dell, but the information gathered by overhearing the officers seemed to her to be of grave importance to the American army. Finally, her plans for the morrow perfected, she sank into a troubled sleep.

Before daylight she was up and on her way to the old house in the woods. Bonny Dell must be fed and watered. She returned and was busy in the kitchen when the captain and lieutenant came down.

As she carried the food to the breakfast table, a sergeant came to inform Lieutenant Bruce that there had been no alarm during the night and that no one had been detected trying to pass the guards.

Captain Meiklejohn talked freely about the plans of the day, and Deborah heard him say that the corvette, *John Adams,* undergoing repairs near Hampden, was to be burned. Her pulse quickened when he told Lieutenant Bruce that Bangor was to be sacked and burned to the ground.

She dared linger no longer. At any moment the captain might question her about Bonny Dell. She almost regretted that she had not ridden away at daybreak, but a moment's reflection told her she had acted wisely. Bonny Dell must be fed before starting, and the vigilance of the soldiers might be relaxed after the coming of day.

She delayed to bid Nancy goodbye, who, if she disappeared without doing so, would be very anxious about her.

Suddenly, Nancy's voice was heard saying, "She is somewhere around the house. I'll find her."

"Tell her I want to see her immediately," the captain said. "If the truth was told me, that white horse would make a gallant charger for an officer of his Majesty's army. Tell her . . ."

His words were lost as Deborah seized the long, homespun riding-skirt from the wooden peg back of the door and ran toward the woods.

A shout caused her to glance behind. A soldier leading two horses had seen the fleeing girl and called to her to stop. But Deborah ran faster than before and had almost reached the woods when she heard the captain shout, "Stop! Stop, I say! Come back here!" A moment, and the sheltering pines hid her from view, but the shouts of the enraged officer still came to her ears.

She was gasping for breath when she reached the old house, where Bonny Dell greeted her with a whinny of delight.

"There isn't a minute to lose!" she exclaimed breathlessly, partly to herself and partly to the horse, as she threw on the saddle and buckled the girth. "There's a cruel man that wants to take you away from me, Bonny, and they are going to surprise the company William is serving in! Just think, Bonny, if anything should happen to William!" Deborah's face was pale as her trembling fingers fastened the bridle. Bonny Dell's delicate muzzle caressed the pale cheek of her mistress, as if to assure her that she would do her best. A moment more and Deborah had donned the brown riding-skirt and sprung into the saddle. For a brief minute she sat with uplifted face; then she leaned over and patted the arched neck. "Bonny," she whispered, "it is for our country and William, and for you, too, dear Bonny Dell!"

The white horse whinnied her answer and trotted down the old woods road by which Deborah hoped to make her way to the high road unobserved.

She reached it in safety, but drew rein suddenly as she remembered that the lieutenant had told the captain that the guards on this road were posted several miles out.

Just what Deborah would have done had she not been alarmed by a hoarse shout will never be known. She looked up the road and saw three men a half mile away, coming at a gallop. She was sure the one in the lead was Captain Meiklejohn, and the second, Lieutenant Bruce. They were seeking Bonny Dell and had doubtlessly already seen the white horse outlined against the dark green pines that fringed the road. Retreat was impossible. There was only one road open, and she must take it or surrender and lose Bonny Dell. In the twinkling of an eye her decision was made. With a touch of her hand and a low word, Bonny was away. The pursuers were gaining, but the white horse broke into a gallop toward distant Hampden.

A glance behind, when a quarter mile was passed, showed that Bonny was holding her own. Deborah's bonnet was carried away by the wind, and her hair was loosened as she rode. Again she glanced behind. The captain, mounted on a great bay horse, was nearer, but Lieutenant Bruce had fallen to the rear, while a soldier rode close behind the shouting, spurring captain.

At that instant she realized that it was not Bonny Dell alone that brought the captain thundering on her trail. It was because he knew that his talk of the night before had been overheard, and that she would alarm the American army if permitted to escape. The thought that the fate of the army was in her keeping crashed upon her with staggering force. For an instant she almost reeled in the saddle; then she leaned far forward and patted the heaving neck. "Bonny! Bonny! Bonny!" she cried. The pink ears slanted back at the well-known voice, Deborah saw the large full eyes turned toward her for an instant; then Bonny's head shot forward as she swept up the road like an arrow from a bow, almost unseating her rider.

Deborah clutched the saddle and leaned low over the laboring shoulders of the flying horse. The long, creamy mane whipped her face, and her own hair streamed behind, a yard-long, blue-black cloud.

"Bonny! Bonny!" she cried. The words, carried by the wind, mingled with the wrathful shouts of the captain. She heard the report of a pistol, and a bullet whistled over her head. Bonny Dell heard it, too, and responded with a burst of speed that left the captain far behind as she dashed up the valley like a white tornado. The slender limbs of the Arabian moved with the regularity and strength of the engine pistons that drive steamers up the historic Penobscot today, as, with outstretched head—her body seeming to skim along the dusty road, foam flecking her sides, and froth flying from distended nostrils—she thundered on.

Three miles! Deborah was far ahead. In her excitement, the soldiers that guarded the road were forgotten until she swung around a curve.

There, a half mile ahead, she saw a sight that filled her with dismay. A group of red-coated men stood, muskets in hands, watching the strange sight that burst upon their vision.

It was not the men only that made Deborah's heart seem to sink in despair. A long pole, shoulder-high, stretched across the road, blocking her path! But no thought of stopping came to Deborah Lee. If Bonny saw the pole, she did not betray her knowledge by faltering. She seemed to quicken her pace as she tore on, and the group in the road gazed in open-mouthed wonder at the spectacle.

"Hit's the hangel o' death!" gasped one, as he watched the oncoming horse and crouching rider.

"Hout o' the road!" roared another, springing to one side; "hit'll go right hover you!"

To either side the soldiers broke, and only those who turned saw Bonny Dell gather herself for the leap. They had a glimpse of a flying, foam-flecked form with streaming mane and tail. They heard the heavy breathing of the snow-white horse and caught a momentary vision of a pale face half concealed by the flowing mane and the gleam of sunlight on Deborah's long hair as Bonny Dell's iron-shod hoofs cleared the pole by a full six inches. When they looked again, horse and rider were disappearing in a cloud of dust far up the road!

A militiaman below Hampden stood aghast as a foaming horse and white-faced rider thundered by unheedful of challenge or man. Sergeant William North heard the sound of galloping hoofs and ran to the roadside. He heard a cry. Deborah had seen him. Before he could realize what it meant, a great white horse, gray now with dust and foam, ploughed up the earth with iron hoofs as Bonny Dell threw herself back on her haunches, and a white-faced girl with flowing hair fell from her saddle crying: "Oh, William! They were going to take Bonny Dell, and they are coming to surprise you and take you all prisoners! I . . . I . . ." Somebody threw his hat in the air and called for three cheers, so that only William heard what followed—unless Bonny Dell heard too, for she raised her head and neighed and caressed Deborah Lee's cheek, rosy once more, with her pink muzzle.

* * * * *

The battle of Hampden was fought and lost. Untrained farmers and clerks were driven back by the flower of the British army. But the sons, grandsons, and great-grandsons of the men who fell back before the bayonets of the invaders at Hampden proved at Antietam and Gettysburg, in Cuba and the Philippines, at Chateau Thierry and in the Argonne, that the blood transmitted to their veins was the red blood of fighting patriots.

Perhaps the ride of Deborah Lee prevented a greater disaster than that which occurred at Hampden on the Penobscot that September day of 1814.

* * * * *

It was a June day the following year when a schooner dropped anchor off Frankfort. Deborah, standing once more in the doorway, wondered at the large number of people gathered to meet the boat that put off from the schooner. The boat was bearing a long, dark box. William North, standing at her side, wondered, too, and so did Nancy Holmes. Even Bonny Dell, grazing nearby, raised her head and gazed curiously at the crowd on the wharf.

That evening, while Deborah sat on a bench in the yard with William at her side, a crowd came marching up the hill to the weather-stained house.

"Why, they are coming here!" Deborah exclaimed.

"So they are, Deb. Looks as if about everybody in town is coming. I wonder what it is they are bringing!"

Before Deborah could answer, the crowd grouped around them. Six men carried the long box that had been taken off the Boston schooner; they advanced and placed their burden on the ground. Then William's former captain stepped forward and said, "The boys of the old company and the people of Frankfort want to give you and Miss Lee something to show what they think of you both. We . . . we sent to Boston and got this. We hope you'll like it. We couldn't think what to get for Bonny Dell."

Someone pulled away the cloth that covered the box; others lifted out a great clock and stood it up before the astonished young people.

It was one of the finest clocks that could be bought in those days. The case was of polished mahogany, and the works bore the name of a famous maker. Above the polished metallic dial was the figure of a galloping horse wrought in silver. On its back it bore the crouching figure of a girl with streaming hair.

William tried to speak, but could not. The tears coursed down his cheeks, and Deborah, at his side, trembled with emotion.

Only Bonny Dell seemed to retain her composure. After the cheers had subsided, and before William North could express the gratitude inspired by the gift, Bonny Dell walked over and gazed at the crowd. Then her eyes rested on the clock a moment, and she raised her head and neighed, as if to show her approval of the entire proceeding.

* * * * *

"The Ride of Deborah Lee," by Chandler Briggs Allen. Published June 1924 in St. Nicholas. *Text owned by Joe Wheeler. Chandler Briggs Allen wrote for popular magazines during the first half of the twentieth century.*

Where Solomon Swapped Horses

H. H. Slawson

When King Solomon's name comes up in discussions, immediately his great wisdom comes to mind, his fabulous wealth, the great temple and palace he built, women like the Queen of Sheba who were in awe of him—but who thinks of horses?

Could it be that horses were the technological revolution of the ancient world?

* * * * *

For three thousand years King Solomon has enjoyed a reputation based upon his wisdom and his wealth. Tales have been spun about his treasures and the places they came from, while the evidence of his intellectual abilities has stood the test of time and still wins admiration everywhere.

Yet somehow, down the ages, the world has lost sight of what must have been, in his day, one of Solomon's outstanding activities. Only brief and scattered mention of it is found in the Old Testament accounts, but archaeological discoveries, lately made, strikingly corroborate these references and impress on us the fact that Solomon was not only the first extensive breeder of fine horses but also the foremost trader in equine flesh. He operated at a time when the horse was almost as novel a sight in Palestine as was the automobile in America a century ago.

For nearly thirty centuries the rubbish has been gathering over the ruins of the fortress city of Megiddo, Palestine's historic Gibraltar, toward the northern end of the Holy Land. In this mound, archaeologists from the University of Chicago's Oriental Institute have been digging to see what the sands of time conceal. And here it was that they brought to light the fallen stone walls of two groups of stables used by the mighty Solomon in his horse-trading business a thousand years before Christ.

From the nearby fields and hillsides, Solomon's barn builders brought the undressed stone that they put into the stable walls. A flat roof was laid above them and covered with mud, while lime plaster was spread as a protective weather coat over the entire structure. The huge barns were built in units. The units adjoined laterally, but there was no way to get from one section to the other inside the building.

Each unit was entered by double doors that swung in small stone sockets, some of which were found still in their original positions. Through these doors one would step into a passageway between two rows of stalls. There were twelve stalls on either side, so that each unit of the barn sheltered twenty-four horses. In the first group of ruins unearthed, there was room for a total of three hundred animals.

Rough stones paved the passageways, and the mangers were large stones hollowed out to hold the hay and grain at feeding time. Unfinished stone pillars to support the roof stood beside each manger, and through these holes had been drilled to be used for the ancient halters.

Grooms walking down the passageways could readily feed their charges, but the awkwardness of the arrangement for bedding and cleaning the stalls is notable. The plan also left no place for storage of hay or grain.

But labor, as has been pointed out, was cheap and abundant in Solomon's day. The labor market being plentifully supplied, it can be inferred that help was also abundant for the care of the horses, so that the inconvenient arrangement of the Megiddo barns probably caused no serious concern.

"Solomon had horses imported from Egypt. . . . Now a chariot that was imported from Egypt cost six hundred shekels of silver, and a horse one hundred and fifty; and thus, through their agents they exported them to all the kings of the Hittites and the kings of Syria" (1 Kings 10:28, 29, NKJV). The business grew swiftly, and soon—as the record states—Solomon was getting his horses out of "all lands" (2 Chronicles 9:28, NKJV). We learn how at one time "Solomon had forty thousand stalls of horses for his chariots, and twelve thousand horsemen" (1 Kings 4:26, NKJV). These he housed in his "chariot cities," (2 Chronicles 9:25, NKJV) which he had caused to be built in various places, some of them, as it now appears, in close proximity to Megiddo. At these localities were accumulated vast stores of "barley and straw . . . for the horses" (1 Kings 4:28, NKJV).

It was only natural that Megiddo should be selected as one of those chariot cities, or depots, where herds of horses could be concentrated and held for disposal among the people to the north of his kingdom. New evidence uncovered by the archaeologists reveals the soundness of his selection.

Historians like to picture Palestine as a bridge over which traders and armies from Egypt, Babylonia, and Nineveh passed and repassed. Right up until recent times, the camel trains of modern merchants have used the same route traversed by those men of vanished ages. Near the modern port of Haifa, this historic highway encounters the white limestone barrier of the Mount Carmel Ridge, and at the pass over this ridge the ancient fortress city of Megiddo was located. Below it lies the plain of Armageddon.

Sifting the soil that covers the ruins of Megiddo, the University of Chicago expedition has gathered a rare hoard of relics that, pieced together, help us form a picture of the life lived in Megiddo long, long ago. Objects salvaged from the dust of the ages make it clear that Megiddo was a cosmopolitan city, frequented by people from many countries. Some of these objects are of Egyptian origin, some came from Greece and the Byzantine area, and still others came from the land of the Tigris and the Euphrates. They represent many periods of time as well as different countries, but it is this notable intermixture of countries and cultures that points to an explanation of why Solomon selected Megiddo as the site of an important horse supply depot. Since all the world converged at Megiddo, was not this a good place for any shrewd business man to set up shop and cultivate an international trade?

A wider and more romantic appeal, however, is inherent in another discovery at the mound. Poking around in the dust of ages, the excavators struck a flight of stairs hewn in solid rock. The steps start at the top of the mound and lead one hundred and twenty feet downward through a shaft that ends in a horizontal tunnel.

Round and round the shaft, the stairs wind for a distance equal to the height of a fair-sized skyscraper. The tunnel at the bottom runs for one hundred and sixty-five feet through solid rock and terminates in a natural cave seventy-five feet long, twenty-five feet high, and fifteen feet wide. At the far end is a spring from which water under the old city site still bubbles.

The entrance to this cave was found on the slope of the hill outside the city, but it had been closed with heavy masonry blocks. Apparently the shaft and tunnel through the rock had been devised for use in time of siege, when it would have been unsafe or impossible to get water through the cave entrance.

When the explorers of this municipal water system reached the far end of the tunnel, they found near the cave entrance the skeleton of a faithful Bronze Age sentry who had died at his post. Beside him lay the bronze head of his spear, the wooden shaft of which had crumbled to dust ages ago. On the rock above his head a patch of soot, still discernible, marked the spot where a torch had once flared and smoked in the darkness.

Examination shows that two gangs of men evidently worked from opposite ends of the 165-foot tunnel to push it through the rock. At the point of juncture there is a slight jog in the wall, indicating that calculations of the ancient engineers worked out very closely. The system was built between three thousand and four thousand years ago, in the pre-Hebrew days of the Canaanite kings. It is recognized as the most extensive engineering achievement of its age yet uncovered in Palestine. The marvel is how it could have been built without the aid of steel or other modern tools.

The Chicago archaeologists have had the stairs repaired and a handrail and electric lights installed so that the visitor to Megiddo today can explore this venerable masterpiece of human ingenuity. As one works his way downward through the shaft, he can fancy himself treading the route Solomon's grooms followed as they toiled to bring up the immense quantities of water which that ancient monarch's horses were always demanding. What a job it must have been!

* * * * *

"Where Solomon Swapped Horses," by H. H. Slawson. Published April 10, 1938, in Young People's Weekly. *Reprinted by permission of Joe Wheeler (P.O. Box 1246, Conifer, Colorado 80433) and Cook Communication Ministries, Colorado Springs, Colorado. H. H. Slawson wrote for popular magazines during the first half of the twentieth century.*

Young Man on the Way Up

Newlin B. Wildes

Dr. Simmons was going to propose, but something went wrong . . . and it was over. One afternoon in November, he went riding.

* * * * *

At four o'clock young Dr. Simmons said goodbye to his last patient with the exact mixture of the personal and professional in his voice to make the patient feel her case was a particularly special one. Young Dr. Simmons was good at that sort of thing. It kept patients coming back, and it made them talk about him to their friends.

Then he went to his desk and looked at the bottom item on his calendar. It said "Dinner—Nancy," but it meant much more than that. It meant his whole life.

He could swing it now, Dr. Simmons thought. He was thirty-three, his office was in the right location, his patients were the right kind, and his professional colleagues, though they might not include him in their more personal parties, respected him. He had never given them a chance to do otherwise. He never would.

Dr. Simmons smiled slightly, and there was a suggestion of human crinkles about his eyes. Then he became serious, reminding himself that one should smile only at the right times. His father, a general practitioner, had smiled too much. He never had collected his bills, and he never had specialized. Young Dr. Simmons was specializing. The throat. That way he built a reputation.

Dr. Simmons got up smartly and shrugged his excellent shoulders into his coat. Tonight was the night.

At 7:29 he parked his shiny black coupe before an old and stately house that made Dr. Simmons appear a little brisk, a little too consciously dressed, as he went up its worn stone steps. He was nervous.

The butler said, "Miss Nancy will be down directly," and showed him into the library—a high-ceilinged, dark-paneled room with a lived-in look. A clock ticked solemnly on the mantel, and a cat regarded Dr. Simmons with green-eyed disapproval from a deep chair.

Dr. Simmons adjusted his tie and put the yellow orchid in its tinselly box on the table. There were quick footsteps on the stair, and a voice said, "Hello, Bill."

Something in that voice picked one up and made one want to laugh. It made young Dr. Simmons smile and brought the crinkles to his eyes and mouth.

Nancy was like the voice. She was small and dark, with a friendly mouth, a little large, but expressive, miraculous lashes, and a strong chin—a girl who would be good on a boat or on horseback, anything that might call for cool thinking. She wore a dull red evening dress that was just right with her smooth shoulders. Young Dr. Simmons gave her the orchid.

"Oooh," she said, "what a nice box! I've seen them in the movies, but I've never had one. And the orchid is lovely, Bill. This is an event."

Dr. Simmons fervently hoped that it was going to be—an event with the right ending. He held her wrap for her.

* * * * *

The Miramar was expensive and good. They had a special table in the corner, and the headwaiter was extremely respectful. Dr. Simmons liked that. Some people he knew saw him, and he liked that, too. The meal was delicious and expensive. Dr. Simmons had thought of everything—he hoped.

He was so much in love with Nancy Carveth that it hurt. He had fallen in love with her when he first saw her at a party, before he had known she was a Carveth with all *that* meant. It meant a lot socially, but it had not made him want to marry her more—or less. This was one thing he did not reason about or care whether it would be good or bad professionally. He was in love just with her.

"I had a wonderful horseback ride this morning," Nancy was saying. "It's such fun in October when it's cool. You haven't been riding lately, have you?"

He came back to things. "I haven't had a minute. Lots of operating and a flood of new patients." He paused, then added too casually, "Today Mrs. Von Lennop brought in her daughter."

Nancy was unimpressed. "A spoiled thing, that daughter."

"But a worthwhile patient," Dr. Simmons reproved gently.

"But Dr. Grandin doesn't care who your patients are, so long as you do some real good!"

He smiled at her. "But I *am* doing good. I—"

She broke in quickly. "But you wouldn't do anything out of the way—anything that might make some fashionable doctors look at you strangely and perhaps talk unfavorably."

His face reddened. "I couldn't afford to do anything that would affect my standing."

She turned away. "That's what I mean. We wouldn't be happy together, Bill."

Her voice was final.

* * * * *

Young Doctor Simmons smiled hardly at all in the days that followed, though business was good and Mrs. Von Lennop sent in some friends who wore handsome furs and had large chauffeur-driven cars. Then one afternoon in November Dr. Simmons appeared suddenly in his waiting room.

"I won't be in this afternoon," he told his receptionist. "You can reach me at Barry Stables if you have to."

Dr. Simmons liked to ride, not fast and furiously, but slowly and lazily and usually alone. Being alone gave him a chance to think, and he particularly wanted to think now. He wanted to convince himself he was right.

Dr. Grandin, of course, could take anyone and everyone for a patient. He already had his reputation. But young Dr. Simmons was on his way up and had to be careful. There were plenty of younger doctors who were eager to laugh at a colleague who got off the beaten track. That sort of thing could

be damaging to a man in Dr. Simmons's position. Nancy Carveth should have seen that. He only wanted to offer her the kind of position she deserved.

But he kept riding during the fall afternoons, and one afternoon he met someone.

The boy was perhaps fifteen and had red hair, a few freckles, a snub nose, and a grin you simply had to return. And he rode an extremely handsome little horse. *A thoroughbred,* Dr. Simmons thought. *Too handsome for a young man in faded dungarees and flannel shirt.*

The boy walked his horse beside Dr. Simmons, and the doctor asked, "Is that your horse?"

The boy nodded, happily important. "A man gave him to me about a year ago. He was a race horse."

* * * * *

They were coming to a fork in the road, and Dr. Simmons thought he might break away. But the boy asked, "You don't mind if I ride with you? I like to ride with someone, and so does Bounder."

"Shall we canter?" the doctor inquired.

"We just walk," the boy said, "and trot sometimes."

"I should think a horse that has raced would love to canter."

"He would love it, and I would, too. But Bounder's got bad wind. When he gallops it hurts awfully. He makes terrible noises, and once he bled. Now we walk."

They walked in silence. "Couldn't you have it fixed?"

The boy shook his head. "It'd cost a lot and be hard to do. A veterinarian told me."

They walked a long way. Then, "Would you canter him a little?" the doctor asked. "I'd like to hear him. I'm a doctor. Not a horse doctor, of course, but I know a little about human throats." He looked at the boy. "Dr. Simmons," he said.

"I'm Jimmy Day," the boy said. "Sure, I'll canter him."

He did, and in 50 yards the wheezing was loud, and the horse's nose was out as he struggled for breath.

"Hm-m," said Dr. Simmons.

At the next fork the boy pulled up. "I have to get home." He hesitated. "I could meet you again tomorrow." The boy's face was hopeful and eager.

"I'd enjoy it," Dr. Simmons said. "Not tomorrow. The day after."

He watched the boy and the horse with the fine legs trot slowly away.

That evening Dr. Simmons sat alone for a while, then went to his library and got some books. He wasn't going to be silly, but there was no harm in satisfying his curiosity. He read till after three. Two days later he saw the boy again.

* * * * *

The boy was glad to see him; so was the little horse. They rode a long time. When they came to a field that was too tempting, the boy said, "You go ahead and gallop. I'll meet you up there."

The doctor let his horse go.

The boy was grinning when they finally came together. "That was pretty, seeing him go," the boy said. "Sometimes I dream that Bounder can gallop through the fields and jump the walls, and his mane is in my face, and he don't wheeze."

The doctor looked at him quickly and looked away.

"I have to get to my chores," the boy said at last. "Would you like to see where Bounder lives?" It was as if the doctor and his horse were his only friends.

"I think I have time," Dr. Simmons said.

A roughly shingled house and tar-papered lean-to stood on the edge of a wood among scrub oak and pine. In the lean-to was a big box stall with good hay. A water bucket hung in the corner.

"Doesn't it cost a lot to keep a horse?" the doctor asked.

The boy nodded. "But I get 50 cents an hour all summer tending lawns, and I have a paper route. Ma knows I like Bounder." The boy grinned, and the little horse pushed against him with its nose.

They love each other, the doctor thought. Aloud he said, "What does your father do?"

"Died in the war. He was just getting this place fixed up. Ma and me and my kid sisters live here now."

Dr. Simmons got back on his horse. "Day after tomorrow, Jimmy?"

* * * * *

That night Dr. Simmons read the same books again. At twelve o'clock he threw them down. "They'll laugh you out of the medical profession," he told himself. "Don't be a fool." And then he remembered Jimmy Day saying, "Sometimes I dream that Bounder can gallop. . . ."

The doctor got up and poked the fire. "No one would have to know," he said. "And I could do it, too."

Two days later, when he met Jimmy again, Dr. Simmons did not waste time.

"Gallop Bounder down the field hard and come back." The boy hesitated. "It won't hurt him."

When the little horse was beside him, breathing hard, fighting for air, the doctor felt quickly, expertly at the throat, both sides, watching carefully. He stood back. "Jimmy, how would you like to have Bounder right, so he could run and jump and play? Would you take a chance to have that?"

The boy looked at him, his eyes large and unsmiling. "You mean it might make him worse?"

"Any operation is a risk. In this case probably not more than one in twenty, if you take care of him." He looked hard at the boy. "I'm a throat doctor. I've been reading up on horses. I'm sure I could do it. Do you want me to try?"

Hopeful tears stood in Jimmy's eyes. "Sure I do, Doc."

* * * * *

There were things to do first, and then the promise. "You must never in any circumstance tell anyone that I did this operation, Jimmy. It would ruin me professionally. My patients would all desert me."

And Jimmy said, "Of course, Doc, but . . ."

"Do you know where we can get a veterinarian who won't talk and who will help with the anesthetic and things?"

Jimmy Day nodded. "I know an old guy. He used to be good, I guess. Now he just sits home and drinks."

Dr. Simmons straightened. "Have him there tomorrow at noon—sober. He won't have much to do."

On that November afternoon in a stall that was clean and bright with the sun, the fashionable young Dr. Simmons, promising throat specialist, performed a delicate operation on a patient named Bounder, who had once been a race horse and now would run through the woods with a boy on his back—a terribly happy boy.

When the operation was done, Dr. Simmons knew his skill had not failed him. He had cut and sewn right, he had found the fault and corrected it. A youngster sat in the shavings of the stall and stroked a lean sleek neck and said "Oh, boy!" over and over.

And a blowzy old man who might once have been a good veterinarian but who now smelled strongly of whisky looked at Dr. Simmons with respect and said, "Doc, that was some job."

Dr. Simmons went back to his apartment, feeling quick and sure and happy and only a little frightened. Nothing, he assured himself, would leak out about this.

* * * * *

But he had a strange feeling when, a week later, he picked up his phone and found that one of the younger doctors, not a friend of his, was calling.

"Hello, Bill," Dr. Barnaby said, "I wonder if you'd help me out?"

"Glad to," Dr. Simmons said carefully.

"You see," Barnaby went on, "my cat has asthma, and I hear you're doing a lot of animal work. . . ."

Dr. Simmons's hand froze to the phone. "Where," he asked coldly, "did you hear that?"

"Some old vet got in his cups and told someone. You know how such things get around. Now this cat . . ."

Dr. Simmons hung up the phone and sat back in his chair. This was the end of everything. It would soon be in every office in town—Dr. Simmons, throat specialist for horses.

Young Dr. Simmons got up slowly and went home. The phone rang. It kept ringing till he took it off the cradle and laid it on the table. He sat in his chair, and the room grew dark and darker. "Kick your career out the window," he groaned.

Then all at once he didn't care any more. He got up and laughed long and loud and began to feel wonderful. The only thing he wanted to do was to go out to Jimmy Day's place and see his patient—perhaps his most important patient.

He felt so free and relieved that when the buzzer sounded, he pressed the button for the downstairs door. When the elevator stopped, he opened the door.

Nancy Carveth came in. She had a fur coat thrown over her shoulders, and her cheeks were bright. "Bill, I've been trying to telephone you. You didn't answer."

"I didn't want to talk to them," he said. "Now I don't care." He replaced the phone. "I suppose you know all about my new patient?"

Nancy Carveth nodded. "Why did you do it, Bill?"

Young Dr. Simmons stopped smiling. "It had something to do with giving someone back his dreams—or part of them."

Then he told her about it, all of it. And Nancy Carveth watched him as he talked. After a while tears gleamed in her eyes. She got up and came to him.

"Ask me again, will you, Bill?" she said. "Won't you ask me?"

Young Dr. Simmons asked her, and she found a satisfactory answer—just as he had found himself.

* * * * *

"Young Man on the Way Up," by Newlin B. Wildes. Published October 1947 in the Family Circle *magazine. Used by permission of Meredith Corporation, publishers of* Family Circle *magazine. Newlin Wildes wrote for mid-twentieth century magazines.*

The Ransomers

Grace Livingston Hill

Mother and Father were at their rope's end. In but a few days the interest payment was due—and if they failed to pay it, they would lose their home. They had nothing else to sell that would bring money enough. Nothing but Old Gray—and he was like a member of the family.

Each day, when the mail failed to rescue them, they died a little. Finally, there was no more time left.

What should they do?

* * * * *

Mother peered anxiously under the old green shade and watched Old Gray come plodding slowly up the road. She strained her eyes and tried to make out from Father's bent attitude whether he was bringing good news or bad, but could not be sure. Then Old Gray passed behind the thick growth of lilac bushes in the front yard, out of sight, and she turned from the window with a sigh.

The simple dinner was all ready, but she had not the heart to take it up till she knew. She opened the door and looked out.

Old Gray, according to habit, stopped in the green drive in front of the stone flaggings, and Father looked up, but he did not smile. The look in his eyes was weary, as if something hurt him.

"Well?" said Mother.

"Nothing from Theodore yet," evaded Father with an attempt at lightness in his voice.

"Didn't the notice come yet?" Mother's voice had a quick catch in it, half impatient at Father's feeble efforts to save her from the truth.

"Yes, it came." Father's voice took on a hopeless note.

"Nothing else in it? You know it's several days late. I didn't know but it might be put off, or the date changed, or something."

"Nothing else, Mother; jest the us'al notice that the int'rest is due the fifteenth o' this month. It's dated jest as us'al. They don't changes dates on things like that, Mother."

Father's tone was gentle, patient, indulgent, as one would explain to a little child.

"Let me see it." Mother put out her hand, and took the envelope eagerly, almost fiercely, as if somehow she might still be able to extract hope from the single sheet of paper folded within.

Father handed it to her with a sigh, and took up the reins.

"Git up!" he said. Old Gray walked staidly, obediently into the barn and drew a sigh of anxiety. He was very susceptible to voices, and he knew something was wrong with the family. Mother usually had a kind word for him, even if there were no apple core or lump of sugar. He loved to nuzzle her worn hand with his old pink nose. The old horse took to his small portion of corn, and ate daintily, reflectively, making it last as long as possible to seem like a big meal, but it did not taste so good as usual. Something was the matter with Mother. And Father! Come to think of it, Father hadn't talked to him nearly so much as usual on the way home from the post office. Something *was* the matter! He took a long breath, and wafted a stray bit of last week's chaff from a corner of the manger, gathered it up carefully with his pink velvet lips, and wished he knew.

Father and Mother ate their meal in silence. There wasn't even any chance to comment on the cooking; for there were only warmed-ups, and Mother didn't say a word about Father not bringing home the things she had told him to get from the store. He had forgotten those, of course, but they could get along without them. With that twenty-five dollars interest money looming ahead, how could they buy such things as sugar and butter?

It was while Mother was washing the dinner dishes that Father, standing by the window, looking down the road, asked quaveringly,

"You don't s'pose Theodore could 'a' forgot the day the int'rest falls due?"

"No, Father; he said it over and over. He said, 'Now, Mother, don't you worry. I'll be sure and have that money here in plenty of time. The fifteenth of September is a long way off, and I'll have the money here by that time!' He marked it down, too."

She wiped her hands on her apron, and went over to the old almanac hanging over the desk in the corner. Adjusting her spectacles, she found the place where a pencil mark testified to Theodore's knowledge of the date.

"Theodore never would let it run this close to the time unless something had happened to him," said Mother, brushing the back of her hand hastily across her eyes.

"Oh, nonsense!" said Father feebly. "Nothing has happened to Theodore, Mother; don't you worry 'bout that. Most likely his letter has miscarried, er else he ain't been able to get the money together es soon es he 'xpected. There couldn't nothing happen to Theodore up there in those big woods in the lumber camp. It ain't like he was in a big city with autymobiles flying round thick."

"A tree could fall on him," said Mother with a catch in her breath as if she had spoken now the awful dread of her heart and almost feared it would bring the calamity.

"Now, Mother, you've jest got to trust in the Lord, and not think o' things like that. You know you promised you would when Theodore had that fine offer and went up there. Moreover, this ain't a time to be thinking of trees falling. We've got that mortgage to pay, an' how we going to do it? That's the question."

They settled down to the inevitable talk which both had known was coming all the week, and both had tried to put off, hoping something would happen to make it unnecessary.

"You don't think 'twould do to tell the man—jest go, explain how 'tis—that Theodore is going to send the money in a few days?"

It was the temptation that had been hovering on the edge of Mother's mind all day; she knew it in the secret place of her soul for the weakness that it was, but somehow it had to come out for Father's condemnation before she could quite get rid of it.

"No, Mother," said Father decidedly, as if he too had thought of that and dismissed it forever. "That wouldn't be businesslike, and 'twouldn't be egzactly honest. What 'd we do ef Theodore didn't get the money? We hev to think of some other way."

"Yes, I s'pose so," sighed Mother, relinquishing the weak way reluctantly. "Well, what are you going to do? Ef Aunt Jane had only left me those spoons instead of leaving 'em to Sara Ann, who didn't need 'em, having plenty of her own, we could mebbe have sold them. They ought to have brought that much; there was two dozen, big and little, and not bent a bit."

"Well, we ain't got the spoons so we won't consider 'em," said Father, impatiently, after the manner of men with the impractical "if onlies" of their women folks.

"Well, you're going to do something, I suppose. Or are you just going to let it alone and have him *foreclose?"* She brought the word out impetuously, that awful word that was like a blow on both their hearts, the fear of which had hung over them for days, ever since they had begun to watch for word from their absent son, and it had not come.

The old man turned his hurt, sorry eyes toward her, and a hard, set look came about his mouth.

"You ain't supposing I've quite took leave of my senses," he said, and then, because she had stung him with the word, he was nerved to say the thing that had been in both their minds for a week. "I don't see nothing for it but to sell the old horse, Mother."

The words were spoken, and they both sat dumb, quivering at the thought. Mother was glad she had not been the one to voice it. She would have had to if Father hadn't done it first; now she felt a strange resentment rising up in her, that he could bear to say it. Old Gray was so like one of themselves. Sell Old Gray!

The tears coursed down her cheeks silently, and her hands dropped helplessly in her lap. The awful thought was out at last. It could be no more hidden in the recesses of their spirits and bidden take leave. It was with them to stay.

The old man cleared his throat several times.

"I know, Mother, I know." He got up nervously and walked over to the window. "I know, it's hard, but I don't see no other way. We've got to be honest, an' we can't let the house go. It's all the place we've got to live in while we stay."

There was silence in the room, save for the soft little sobbing sound of Mother's breath. The old cat realized that something was the matter and got up from the mat by the stove, going over to Father and winding herself lovingly about his feet. She purred loud comfort as well as she knew how, but there were tears on Father's face and in his eyes. He could not see out the window. The lilac bushes were blurred upon the pane, and he could not see the cat when he tried to look down.

Supper that night was a mere ceremony which each got through somehow for the sake of the other, and bedtime, though welcome, did not bring relief. Neither slept at all, and about four o'clock in the morning Mother said quaveringly, out of the flatness of her damp pillow, "We'd have to be sure he had a good home."

"Of course," said Father briefly, and silence reigned again till five o'clock, when Father got up and hurried out to the barn. He had purposely fed Old Gray after dark the night before. He couldn't bear to look the kind old horse in the face. Both he and his wife had been conscious all night of the animal's presence out there, as if he were another human being lying awake and wondering why they acted so strangely toward him—he who had been a faithful part of the family for so many years.

There was very little corn left in the bin, but Father gave Old Gray an extra helping that morning, and patted him on the nose as if ashamed. Then he bolted from the barn.

When he came into the house, Mother looked up anxiously from the mush she was frying as if to ask whether Father had told Old Gray and how he took it. But Father only blew his nose hard and went and looked out the window.

Three days they stood the agony, going through the forms of eating and sleeping without the spirit, and both were overborne with sorrow. Twice each day Old Gray plodded to the post office two miles away, and Mother went along. She felt as if she couldn't bear to lose a single ride now with the old horse, there were so few left. With a pang she watched his bony body plod along ahead.

Each time the post office came in sight new hope sprang up in their hearts, only to die away in utter sadness when Father came out empty handed.

The road lay along the old canal, and usually Mother loved the view—the bright, still water with its green banks and purpling hills in the distance. She usually looked back at the turn of the road to get another glimpse of the white church-spire back in the village. But that day the tears hid water, hills, and green banks alike, in one misty blur.

At a little roadside store on the outskirts of the village Father drew up and began to speak to the man who reclined against a barrel in front of the door.

"Say, Dave, d' ye know anyone wants to buy a horse?"

Mother quivered at the words, and neither of them dared look at Old Gray, who turned an inquiring eye around at the words, and drew a long sigh of astonishment. So it had come to that!

Dave Hardy shifted his position against the barrel, crossing the other foot over, took in the outfit with a final, lingering, comprehensive glance at Old Gray, and replied at leisure, "Wall, I dunno. Yeh might try Lym Rutherford. He's gen'ally ready fer a good bargain in horseflesh. That the horse? He's gettin' on in years, ain't he?"

"He's not so old," said Father with asperity. "He's got a good deal of spirit left in him yet. I was thinking of Rutherford. Git up, Gray!" And Old Gray, always ready to play up to the part assigned, threw up his ragged tail and pranced off at quite a lively pace considering his heaviness of heart. But Mother leaned back toward the man on the barrel and called anxiously, "Is he kind, Mr. Hardy? Is Mr. Rutherford kind to his horses?"

"Wall, now," laughed Dave Hardy, "I never considered that he made a specialty o' kindness t' anythin' but himself, but I guess he's as kind as the gen'ral run of 'em." And Mother had to be content with that.

They drove straight to Lyman Rutherford's farm, a mile and a half from their own home.

"Guess we better get it over with, hadn't we, Mother?" asked Father as they turned into the road that led to the Rutherford farm.

Mother wiped her eyes and nodded. She had no more words left.

When they drove into the lane by the house, Lyman Rutherford was standing in the open barn door with two other men—a neighbor and a hired man. Father got out and left Old Gray standing by the house, with Mother sitting under her umbrella in the buckboard, her heart beating like a trip hammer. Father walked slowly, determinedly down to the barn. He wanted to get the preliminaries over out of Mother's hearing. It was hard for Mother. Men had to bear such things, but women somehow couldn't.

Mother sat holding on to her umbrella and trying to keep from trembling. She was afraid Mrs. Rutherford might be at home and come out to talk to her, but no one came, and the minutes passed. A great Newfoundland dog lay on the porch as if he were set to guard the house, and the hens clucked about in the lane noisily. Mother found herself wondering how they could bear to make such ugly, contented sounds. She watched the four men in the distance and wondered just what Father was saying, half hoping that Mr. Rutherford would say, "No" at once and end the agony. Then a panic seized her lest he would, for how could they pay the interest if they did not sell Old Gray?

As if to give Father an opportunity to talk with Lyman Rutherford, the hired man and the neighbor sauntered leisurely up the lane to Old Gray and began to examine him critically, taking no further notice of Mother than to pull their old hats half off and jam them on again. They became at once absorbed in the horse.

They pointed out the lame spot on his leg where an old swelling sometimes showed itself and gave a limping gait to the beast. They slapped his sides in what seemed a most unnecessarily cruel manner, making the dignified old horse start and quiver as if the contact hurt his spirit rather than his body. Then the neighbor seized his kind pink nose roughly, and, holding him uncomfortably by the under lip, forced his mouth open to examine his teeth. It appeared that they were telling his age in some mysterious way by this indignity, and Mother sat as quietly as she could, trying to control her wrath and her anguish, her mild eyes snapping with indignation.

It seemed ages to Mother that the men poked and mauled and slapped the beloved Old Gray, muttering half-laughing jokes about his ribs and his years, but at last they turned and went back to the barn, and a conference was held by the three men. Father came hurriedly and stood beside Old Gray, touching him gently here and there, as if to find out whether he had been hurt and to try to explain or make up to him for the insults he had suffered.

There followed a period of silence and waiting. Mother didn't dare say a word, and Father didn't dare look at her. It seemed like the awful silence that precedes a funeral service.

Then Mr. Rutherford came forward, the other two men following slowly.

"Wall, I'm willin' to give twenty-five dollars, no more, fer the hawse, an' I'll add five more fer the waggin ef you want to sell it. It ain't wuth much to me. In fact, I don't need any more *ve*hikels 'bout the place, but to 'commodate you I'll give you five dollars fer it."

Father looked helplessly at Mother, whom tears and anger were beginning to threaten, but, when they turned to each other for support in resisting this old skinflint, lo! There rose up between them the stern wall of necessity, and each saw in the eyes of the other the fatal words: "We must! It is probably the best we can do!"

"Wall, I'll take it," at last said Father, his voice choking miserably as he turned away to hide his emotion.

"You'll find you've got a good market price," said the bargain-maker, stooping to look at Old Gray's lame foot.

Father did not reply.

"You'll want to take your wife home, I s'pose," said Lyman Rutherford, looking up in the uncomfortable silence.

But Mother arose in her might and began climbing down to the ground.

"No, I'll walk," she said decidedly. "We'll have it over with. I couldn't stand it to take him home again, Father."

Father wheeled sympathetically. "Ain't you 'fraid it 'll be too much fer you, Mother? It's a good mile and a quarter from here."

"No, I got to get used to walking. I might as well begin," Mother said decidedly. Father knew it was no use to argue when Mother spoke like that.

Mother walked straight up to Old Gray and put her hand on his kind, old face. He leaned his head down to her affectionately, and she laid her cheek against his nose for a minute and closed her eyes. Then she turned with a quick catch of her breath like a sob and started off down the lane. Mr. Rutherford looked after her a moment furtively and began fumbling in his pocket. He took out a roll of ragged bills, and counted out thirty dollars, handing them over to Father, who took them without a word and hurried after Mother as if ashamed. He felt as if he had sold one of the family. He did not turn to look at the horse, whose kind eyes watched him forgivingly as he went down the lane, as if he understood the necessity.

When the old couple were out of hearing, Lyman Rutherford chuckled amiably. "Beats all what fools women is with animals and children," he remarked and then turned toward the horse with a strange feeling that he had been overheard by one of the family.

"Guess I was a fool fer buyin' 'im," he said reflectively, kicking at Old Gray's fore hoof. "But mebbe I kin fatten 'im up an' sell 'im over in the next county for a lady's drivin' hawse. Ladies don't know much 'bout age."

Father and Mother walked silently down the lane and into the road. Mother was crying, and Father was not far from it. They said not a word to each other, but plodded on in the hot sunshine. When they had gone about two-thirds of the way, Mother was almost exhausted.

"Sit down and rest a few minutes, Mother. Here's a nice place on the bank all shaded by that haystack. You're all beat out."

Father helped her, and she sank down on the bank exhausted and sobbed a minute or two.

"Seems like I just couldn't bear it!" she said, trying to hold the tears back again, for she saw how hard it was for Father. "While you was bargaining, I got to thinking how Old Gray stopped stock still and looked round at our little Betty that time she was riding him bareback, an' fell off. That was two years 'fore she died. He was young and coltish then, an' he might a killed her; but he didn't! An' now we've gone an' sold him fer twenty-five dollars to pay off a miserable little interest on a mortgage. Seems turrible. I don't know what Theodore'll say when he comes home. He meant to send that money. We might a waited another day. P'raps his letter'll come by morning with a check."

"I know, Mother; but that int'rest had to be paid, an' there's only one more day. We couldn't wait. It's hard, but there wasn't nothing else to do."

"It seems awful, jest fer that little money, an' he having our Old Gray. You could see he wasn't caring a bit about him. He jest cared how much he'd be worth to him. And our comfortable buckboard going for five dollars! It's dreadful. How can we go to church?"

"Never mind, Mother, bear up! Bear up! I know it's hard; but mebbe Theodore'll make money up there in the lumber camp an' come home an' buy you a new one some day."

"I don't want a new one. I want the old one we saved and scrimped to buy. It suited me better 'n any autymobile could. And I want our old horse!"

"Yes, yes, Mother. Bear up! Mebbe Theodore'll be able to buy Old Gray back."

"Old Gray may be dead by that time," sobbed Mother, utterly giving way now. "He can't stand hard treatment and hard work. He's old. They said it, and he is. He'll die of a broken heart."

"Now, now, Mother," comforted Father; but his own heart was almost broken. Now on the offside of that haystack, well sheltered from observation, sat three boys who had been resting from their morning's play, dozing in the shade of the haystack. Not wanting to reveal themselves at first, they had remained quiet as the old couple had arrived, and now the three were obliged to listen. Perhaps there could not have been found three more uncomfortable boys in the county than they were as they endured Mother's sobs and Father's feeble attempts to comfort her. Gradually, the whole story crept down the sensitive spine and into the alert young mind of each boy and stirred his emotions as he never would have allowed them to be stirred if he could have helped it. Yet they could not get away.

Three dusty, red-faced boys crept out at last from under the straw, and looked furtively down the road after Father and Mother.

"Ain't that fierce?" said "Spud" Smith as he mopped his brow with his shirt sleeve.

"Fellers, that gets my goat! D' ye know who they are?" asked James Leander Richardson, otherwise known as "Leany Rich."

"Who are they?" said "Beany" Johnson, leaning around the haystack to see better. "Why, they're Ted Brown's folks!"

"That's right! So they are! Ain't that fierce?"

There was silence for half a minute.

"Who'd they say bought that horse? Rutherford? Jest like him. He's an old skin flint. Say, let's go up an' have a look at the horse."

They scrambled down the bank and were off silently, hands in their pockets, kicking the dust viciously now and then by way of easing their emotions. Scarcely anything was said on the way.

They skirted the surrounding fields until they reached the old pasture. Yes, there he was, Old Gray, standing alone in the pasture, looking reflectively over the bars at the cows in the next meadow. Old Gray was not enjoying his chance to eat the grass that grew plentifully about him. He was looking off into space, meditating on the sad ways of life. He was trying to understand. His thin face, visible ribs, and lean haunches all showed that his had not been a life of luxury. His kind eye told that he was ready for whatever sacrifice might be demanded of him.

The boys mounted the fence, took out their knives, and began to hack at the top rail, watching the old horse silently. At last Spud spoke.

"Say, fellers, let's can that deal. Ted would feel something awful. 'Member the flies he used to knock out to us down on the old ball field? He sure was the best coach we ever had."

"No chance!" said Beany decidedly. "We'd just get canned ourselves fer swipin' him. What good 'ud that do, Brownie?"

"Aw, what 'r yeh givin' us? I don't mean swipe him. Course we'd get pinched if we did that. I mean *buy* him, out 'n' out, like anybody."

"*Buy* him!" sneered Beany. "Quit yer kiddin'! How could we?"

"Buy him!" screamed Leany. "Own him an' ride him! Wouldn't that be some class? We could keep him out in our old machine shop."

"Not buy him fer ourselves, y' poor dunce!" Spud's indignation fairly exploded, and he punctuated his words with a thrust in Leany's ribs. "Can't yeh ever see anything but yerself? What 'ud Brownie think o' you, my son, if he was to come back an' find you ridin' round on his dad's horse? No, sir! We're going to buy him an' send him back to 'em safe an' sound."

"Where'll yeh get the money?" demanded Beany. "I ain't got but a nickel, an' I owe that to Jonesey."

"Easy 'nough," said Spud with assurance. "I know where we can get a job right off, an' we'll buy the horse on th' 'nstalment plan, a few dollars at a time. We'll likely have to raise a little on the price, 'r he won't sell. Come on; we've got to hustle 'r he'll sell him to someone else mebbe, an' anyhow we want to get it back to 'em 'fore Brownie gets home again."

The boys obediently descended from the fence and followed their leader through the pasture, down the road, and into the village at a lively pace, Spud dilating as he went on the possibilities of labor and wages for the three.

To his own back yard he led them, where was a great pile of old iron, wire, nails, and tin roofing.

"There!" said Spud, waving his arm dramatically over the field of action. "There's yer work. Dad said last week if I'd have that sorted an' take it down to the foundry before next week, he'd give me three dollars. We c'n get it all done 'fore dark if we work hard. We gotta rake up the yard, too. Then we'll take that money up to Rutherford t'night if it ain't too late, an' pay the first 'nstalment. Come, get to work!"

"All that? We can't ever get that done!" groaned Leany, bracing himself against the weathered fence and looking discouraged.

"Mebbe you don't want to be in this combination?" threatened the demagogue darkly. " 'Cause, if you don't, there's plenty o' friends of Brownie's we c'n get dead easy. Can't we, Beany? Say the word. D' you want to 'r don't yeh?"

If Spud had held a revolver in his face, Leany could not have straightened up quicker.

"Sure! I'll do it," he said in quite an altered tone.

"Well, get to work then; we ain't got any time to lose. You take wire. It's easiest." There was a covert sneer in his tone which completely finished poor lazy Leany. "Beany c'n take nails an' iron, an' I'll take tin; there's more o' that 'n anything else. Put 'em in piles. Beany, put the nails on the porch. Leany, you stack the wire by the fence here, an' I'll pile the tin down by the gate. I'll take the first wheelbarrow load to the foundry an' 'xplain, an' you hev a lot gathered up time I get back. Hustle now. See which c'n get his heap biggest." With the skill of a born contractor he marshaled his forces, and soon the back yard began to look like a junk shop. But load by load it was hurried away to the foundry in the wheelbarrow by three excited boys, urged on by a furious driver who had no mercy.

As they returned from their last trip, dirty, weary, and hungry, triumph in their eyes and a thought of supper in their minds, helped on by the savory odors that were floating on the village air, Spud halted in front of a house where a generous sprinkling of new bright shingles on the roof showed that repairs had just been finished.

"Here's where we get our next job," said Spud with satisfaction in his voice. "Come on in. We better see about it now." He swung the gate open.

"No chance!" declined Leany. "I'm tired, and, besides, we ain't got that yard raked up yet. Come on; I gotta get home. It's supper-time."

Spud stood grimly in front of him, a smear of iron rust across his fierce young face. "Are you goin' to turn yellah? 'Cause, ef you are, now's the time. There comes Pete, an' Jonesey lives just up the street. They're pretty good frien's of Brownie's."

Leany turned without a word. He was weary, but he was not "yellah." Spud was in earnest, and Pete was an old enemy of whom Leany was deeply jealous. He stood without further protest while Spud made the contract for cleaning up Miss Lamson's yard.

"We'll make it fine es silk fer a dollar and a half," said the young contractor, mentally estimating how long it would take and how many shingles there were to be picked up.

"Will you pile the shingles neatly by the kitchen door?" asked Miss Lamson doubtfully.

"Sure," said Spud.

"Could you possibly get it done by tomorrow noon? I'm going to have the Aid Society here in the afternoon, and I'd like it to look nice."

Spud shook his head doubtfully, then brightened into a winning smile as if a happy thought had struck him.

"You couldn't make it two dollars?" he said insinuatingly. " 'Cause then I could get another feller to help, an' we'd get it done sure."

"Why, yes, I'd pay two dollars if it was all done by one o'clock," she said.

"Then we'll be here at seven o'clock in the morning," said the contractor and marched out, followed by his meek supporters.

"For the love o' Mike, Spud, seven's awful early. Can't yeh make it eight?" protested Beany when they were out in the street.

But Leany was looking across the street at Pete and wondering who that "other feller" was likely to be.

"Say, Spud, I guess we could get along, us three alone, ef we began that early," he said.

"Sure!" said Spud easily, looking his satisfaction furtively at Leany. "I meant to all th' time, Leany; only I wanted more money. No, Beany; we gotta get another job fer the afternoon so we gotta get this one done."

"Say, now, Spud, this is vacation," growled Beany, but was stopped by the sudden appearance of Spud's father, from whom the young contractor demanded his pay.

They followed Mr. Jones back to the yard, finished raking it, and received three crisp new dollars, after which neither Leany nor Beany made further protests, but gathered up their stiff limbs and hurried home for supper, agreeing to meet Spud and go out to Rutherford's to see about the horse.

Scrubbed and shining they appeared at the farmer's back door an hour and a half later, and made their astonishing proposition to buy Old Gray, harness and outfit, for thirty-five dollars, on the installment plan, producing their three new dollars to bind the bargain.

Lyman Rutherford had heard of several young horses which were for sale cheap over in the next county and was already sorry for his purchase of the afternoon. He was too shrewd a man not to see an advantage in the boys' proposition. At least, he would lose nothing by it. If the boys were foolish enough to want the horse, it was nothing to him. He agreed that, when they had paid ten dollars, they might take the horse away, bringing at least a dollar a week thereafter, and promptly, until the amount was all paid.

"We gotta get more fellers into this, I guess," said Spud doubtfully as they stood outside under the stars once more. "We gotta make this thing go now, and we must have that ten dollars by Saturday. Brownie might come back most any time now."

"Jes wait awhile, an' see what we c'n do," said Leany eagerly. "An', anyhow, let's not have Pete 'r Jonesey. They always want to run things."

"We'll see," said the boss briefly. "Come on now; we'll go an' have a look at *our horse.*"

Silently they stole around the house, across the barnyard to the pasture fence and down through the pasture to where Old Gray was spending his first night for years under the stars without care or keeping, the dews of heaven upon his patient gray head.

It is curious what a feeling of proprietorship will do. Old Gray had suddenly become to the eyes of those boys the most beautiful horse that ever cropped pasture, and they stood around him, admiringly telling over his good points in a low tone and touching him almost reverently. Who shall say that those rough, kindly young hands did not comfort the spirit of the lonely old horse on the hillside that first night of his exile?

The days passed, and vacation was slipping away unnoticed. The boys were having the time of their lives, working with mysterious zeal. The other boys of the village couldn't understand it and weren't allowed in the combination despite their most wily attempts, for Leany was "making good," and Spud meant to let him have his way as long as he came up to scratch.

"I'm sure John's up to some mischief or other, Papa," said Spud's mother anxiously. "He comes home terribly dirty every night and goes to bed without my saying a word. I haven't had to call him to breakfast once this week. Maybe you better speak to him. I'm real worried about him."

"Let him alone," said Spud's father. "He's only got something on his mind. Pity he wouldn't keep it there and help him get up mornings."

The jobs hadn't all been so plentiful or so remunerative as on the first two days, and the boys had to work hard and pick up little errands here and there. Fifty cents, a dime, a nickel—they all counted. No more candy or soda; they couldn't spare the money. Even gum was taboo. They worked night and day whenever they could find anything that paid. They had hoped to be able to pay the ten dollars by Sunday night and take their horse away,

but there were no more three-dollar jobs, or even two-dollar ones, and the yards and gardens seemed to be singularly well cared for around their neighborhood. However, they did not lose heart, and Sunday night, counting up, they found they lacked only seventy-five cents of completing the first ten-dollar payment.

"My grandmother promised me a dollar once if I would learn the books of the Bible. I know 'em all but the minor prophets," confessed Leany reluctantly.

"You're the stuff, Leany!" cried Spud, slapping him on the shoulder. "Learn 'em, old boy! The rest of us'll get a quarter apiece at least somehow, and we'll get some corn to put in the wagon. We'll go get the corn now out o' this money, an' then you go home an' learn them prophets. We'll pay fer the horse t'night, an' in the morning we'll take a little joy ride out toward the crossroad. Then in the afternoon we'll put the corn in the wagon and take him home. School begins Monday, but we sure can earn that dollar a week fer a while. I bet I c'n make two dollars a week easy."

They carried out their plan, but not the least hard of all the tasks of the week was that of James Leander Richardson, sitting heavy-eyed and stolid beside his astonished grandmother, learning the names of the minor prophets!

Monday morning dawned bright and clear, and the boys were astir early. Spud did not wait for breakfast, but took a piece of cornbread and slid out. Eagerly the three took their way to the Rutherford farm and presented themselves to receive their property, assuring Lyman Rutherford that the weekly installments would be paid regularly. Gravely they took the harness and climbed the pasture fence. Old Gray received them almost effusively. He had been lonely that long week, and sad thoughts had dwelt with him. He bowed his neck to the bit, and walked majestically behind the boys to the barn where the buckboard stood. Almost reverently the boys lifted the shafts, and buckled him in. Their own horse, bought and partly paid for by the honest sweat of their brows! It was almost too much to believe!

They climbed into the buckboard and picked up the reins. Spud, of course, was to drive first.

Old Gray seemed to realize what was happening, and, lifting up his fine gray head, lit out over that country road as if it had been a racecourse and he a blooded courser.

Perhaps the week in the fresh air had done him good or the break in the monotony had lifted his hope and given him new strength. Whatever it was, he certainly did set a tremendous pace that morning for a staid old horse. Perhaps his grateful heart thought he was rendering service in taking the boys over the hills and valleys that beautiful September morning, but he seemed to enjoy it as much as the boys, whose eyes sparkled and whose shouts rang out on the air gayly. For that one morning Old Gray was their own horse, and rightfully. It was all they were asking for their hard task, but it was enough, and they meant to enjoy it to the full.

After dinner, when the dishes were washed up and everything was quiet, Mother put on a clean white apron and sat down in the big rocker by the desk. Father drew up the rush-bottomed chair with the patch-work cushion, and sat beside her.

In the desk behind Mother was the receipt for the interest on the mortgage. The house was safe, but the old horse was gone from the barn, and every one of them, even the cat, was conscious of the sadness that brooded over the whole place.

Father opened his newspaper and read while Mother closed her eyes, trying to listen and not think of the empty barn and the dear boy far away who had not written when he said he would.

Old Gray approached his home from the upper road that could not be seen from the window that looked down the road. Softly the boys stole up to the house to reconnoiter. They crept behind the lilac bushes around the house, and Spud shinnied up a tree a little back from the window till his eyes were on a level with Father's gray head and he could see Mother sitting with her eyes closed. The sight of it all was enough for Spud, and he slid softly down the tree with a mist upon his eyes. Not even the cat, dozing in her ample furs by the stove and pretending to listen, had caught a glimpse of him. The look on his face when he came down to the ground and muttered, "They're there all right!" made the other two boys curious, yet almost afraid to look, and each came down with that same awe over him.

They led Old Gray slowly, softly into the green drive. It was like a triumphal pageant. The basket of corn was in plain sight on the seat, a whole bushel, besides some oats in a box and a little hay under the seat. Around Old Gray's neck, hung like a gigantic locket, was an old pasteboard box cover on which was painfully inscribed, *"I have bought myself back and have come home to stay."*

By the stone flagging at the side door, where Mother always got into the buckboard, the old horse stopped of his own accord. Then Spud, because of his leadership, gave three loud knocks on the door, and the boys fled around the corner of the house and lay flat behind some alder bushes.

What they saw and heard that day as they lay behind the alders peering out, the three boys will never tell. They never even spoke of it to one another. They crept away when all was safe and quiet and Father had ceased to look for any one who might have brought the horse back. The look on each boy's face was as if he had gazed into the depth of two human hearts and learned a great deal of life.

Six weeks later Theodore came home in a panic from the lumber camp to see what was the matter with Father and Mother. His letter and check had been returned to him from the Dead-Letter Office. His writing was atrocious sometimes; that's a fact. And he could pitch a ball better than address an envelope.

All that Lyman Rutherford had told Father was that a couple of boys had bought the horse on the installment plan, and he didn't know them nor know as he'd recognize them if he saw them again. It was nothing to him as long as he got his money.

But, when Ted Brown got home, things began to be found out, and it wasn't long before Ted had the three culprits, as sheepish for all the world as if they had stolen Old Gray, and was telling them what he thought of them.

"Great work, old man, great work!" said the former coach, gripping Spud's grimy hand. "You're right there with the goods and no mistake about it. You're all right, every one of you, and I sha'n't forget it of you. You've made a home run, and I'm proud of you!"

He gave them their money back, and associated with them freely before the jealous eyes of the other boys. And, when Ted left them, Leany looked down at the roll of bills in his hand exultingly.

"Wow!" he said reflectively. "Say, we was workin' fer ourselves, after all, wasn't we? Ain't that great?"

* * * * *

Sometimes in his stall when he is wakeful Old Gray remembers his exile in the pasture and the three silent visitors under the starlight, who stroked his old lonely coat and made him feel better. He sighs contentedly, for he feels that his time of sacrifice is over and home is good at last.

* * * * *

"The Ransomers," by Grace Livingston Hill. Included in Hill's 1949 anthology, Miss Lavinia's Call and Other Stories. *Reprinted by permission of Robert Munce. Grace Livingston Hill (1865–1947) was one of the most prolific authors in American history. Her works have remained popular for most of a century.*

When Kindness Paid

Ruth Foltz

So badly was Bogus hurt that it was decided to put him out of his misery—but Winifred had other ideas.

Little did she then realize the forces she'd set in motion.

* * * * *

The herd of horses lifted their heads from the dry grass they were eating and sniffed the hot July air. Down the winding path a man was slowly approaching. The leader, Bogus, snorted as the man spoke softly.

"Come, Prince. Here, Prince. Come, Prince. Come, Prince. Whoa!"

Two more steps, and the large white horse would have been caught, but at that moment Bogus, with another snort, whirled and was off down the hill like a shot, the others at his heels.

It was fully a half mile to the river, and the hill was so steep Austin wondered that the horses did not stumble and fall. Patiently he started after them, glad that he was following them down instead of up the hill. Suddenly he paused. There was a scream and a cloud of dust, and the bay leader was down. The others scattered and stopped. Austin hurried to where Bogus lay gasping and struggling and saw a great, gaping wound between his forelegs where the horse had harpooned himself on an old fence picket.

"Too bad, old boy, but I'm afraid you've had it coming to you for a long time. That will be the end of you, I'm afraid."

At the dinner table he told the ranch owner what had happened. The other men agreed that it was a good thing that it was Bogus, the outlaw and troublemaker, and not a better horse. But throughout the tale, Winifred Morley sat speechless, her eyes wide and sympathetic, until at last she heard her uncle say, "What did you do with him, Austin? Is he still alive?"

"Yes, but he won't live long, probably. I'll go down and shoot him after dinner. I didn't have a gun with me this morning."

"Yes," agreed his employer, "that is a good idea. Put him out of his misery."

"But why shoot him, Uncle Ben? Let me have him if you don't want him!" Winifred begged.

"Oh, no! Why, I'd be afraid to have you go near him even now. He'd probably bite an arm off you. No, let him go. You can ride Prince and the others all you wish," replied the girl's uncle with finality.

But the sixteen-year-old Winifred pleaded on, till at last he consented. The rest of the afternoon she was busy carrying bandages, disinfectant, and drinking water to the sick horse, and rigging up an old canvas to keep the flies off. Tenderly she dressed the wound with gentle fingers, crooning to Bogus all the while.

For many days she cared for him, then finally one morning she rode him into the corral. The men gathering for breakfast, saw her and gasped, for none but the most daring among them had ever ridden this horse, and then not for long, as he was a vicious bucker and usually ended the performance by rearing up and falling over on his side. But now he walked quietly into the corral and stood while Winifred slid off his bare back.

Quickly the men gathered around, though not too close.

"Yo're takin' yore life in yore tew hands, a-ridin' that varment, Miss!" remarked Charlie gravely.

"Do you think so?" replied the girl, smiling proudly. "Here, Bogus, shake hands!"

The horse lifted a foreleg toward her hand, and she shook it and patted him.

"Now kiss me!" And while the men watched with memories of sharp nips this horse had given them, Bogus brushed her cheek with his soft nose. There were one or two more tricks, then she gave him some sugar and tied him up.

"How did you do it? You must have started in on the day he was hurt." Uncle Ben's eyes were full of admiration for his niece, who had been the madcap of the place since she had come at the beginning of the summer, a thin girl from the city, to gain health and strength at her uncle's ranch. From the day of her arrival, she had ridden the horses without the formalities of saddle or bridle; had galloped them out into the middle of the river and then dived from their backs, coaxing them with sugar cubes to come back to her; then had dashed up and down the river bar on them. Many falls had failed to shake her ardor, though her uncle had said that he would be white-haired before she was through.

Now she smiled at him, proudly.

"I *did* start in as soon as he was able to stand up," she admitted. "By that time he had lost all fear of me, and he has been as gentle as a kitten ever since. These moonlit nights, I have been taking him down to the river bar and teaching him tricks and fancy steps. He has wonderful endurance and endless energy."

* * * * *

Autumn deepened into winter, and the rains came. After a particularly long and heavy storm, Winifred was impatient to get her mail. No one had been out to the post office for some time.

"But we can't get it today, and probably not for a week or two," her uncle protested. "The river is way up, and there isn't a boat in the country. You'll just have to get used to being patient. You are living in pioneer country now, you know, not in town."

But Winifred was *tired* of being patient! She knew that it was useless to say more, but after the men had gone about their various duties, she bridled and saddled Bogus, which she seldom did, and started off.

"Where are you going?" asked Aunt Sarah apprehensively.

"I am going after the mail," replied the girl, and she was gone before her horrified aunt could recover her speech. For a moment the older woman thought frantically, but it was no use; the men were far away, and there was no horse available for her to use in pursuit, and the girl would have almost reached the river already. Then a brighter thought came. Bogus would refuse to attempt to cross the river even for Winifred. Thus comforting herself, she returned to her work.

And Bogus indeed refused to cross the river! At last, Winifred decided that her only chance lay in swimming across. She wound the bridle end around her wrist and started out, wading as far as possible into the muddy, rushing waters.

"Why, it isn't half bad!" she said to herself, thinking she must have found a better crossing than usual. But at that moment she put her foot down into a deeper channel amid the rocks, and a mighty force seemed to grip her ankles, twisting, pushing, throwing her down, and splashing roughly over her face. She felt herself hurled against a large rock, pulled back, and hurled again. Fighting the whirling waters, she raised her head and got her breath. Around her were a semicircle of rocks, their slippery sides sloping toward her, making it impossible to grasp them or pull herself out. She knew she could not hold out long, and realized that she could make no headway against the current, try as she might.

Then, as the world was beginning to grow dim and unreal before her eyes, a dark head appeared over the edge of one rock. Bogus! Winifred let the waters hurl her against the rock again, and seized the dangling bridle. Again the waters hurled, and Bogus pulled, dragging her over the rock and into shallow water. But she could not rise. Bogus put an inquisitive nose down, and she clasped her arms around his neck. He threw back his head, and together they stumbled ashore, Winifred hanging onto a stirrup to keep from falling down again.

Back on solid ground again, she buried her face on his neck as they both panted for breath.

"For," she said, as she retold the tale to me many years later, "you see it was 'turnabout's fair play.' I had saved his life, and now he had saved mine!"

* * * * *

"When Kindness Paid," by Ruth Foltz. Published July 21, 1936, in The Youth's Instructor. *Reprinted by permission of Joe Wheeler (P.O. Box 1246, Conifer, Colorado 80433) and Review and Herald® Publishing Association, Hagerstown, Maryland. Ruth Foltz wrote for inspirational magazines during the first half of the twentieth century.*

Match Race

Walter Farley

Untold millions of us, during our growing-up years, have read Walter Farley's Black Stallion books, thus they can justifiably be labeled "right of passage books"—unthinkable for a horse-loving child or youth to grow up without Farley's imprint on his or her mind.

In this account (taken from The Black Stallion Revolts*), the series hero, thanks to an accident, has amnesia and thinks his name is McGregor. As the horse race proceeds, the boy's memory comes back.*

* * * * *

Allen didn't step away from the black stallion. Instead he reached for the bridle. He'd never before taken hold of the stallion, but in his great excitement he didn't think of this now. For the moment he'd forgotten all caution. He was thinking only of the race to come, the race that a few minutes ago had been hopelessly lost to him. Now he was taking *his entry* to the post. The crowd was waiting for them. After the race he'd do all he could for McGregor. But he needn't think of that now. He turned to the sheriff. "Tom," he said, "you'll find a racing whip in the tack trunk. Please get it for me." He began walking.

The boy hardly breathed; his head reeled when his horse stepped forward obediently beneath Allen's hand. This wasn't as he'd planned. The stallion was eager to go along with Allen. McGregor sat back in the saddle, his spine stiff. He could do nothing but await an opportunity to be free of Allen. He rose in his stirrups and leaned forward again, talking to the stallion, reminding him that he was there. But the small head never tossed or turned in understanding of his sounds and touches. There was no flicking back of pricked ears to listen to him. The stallion's senses were keyed to what lay ahead.

Allen kept walking, taking them ever closer to the track. The boy saw the faces of the crowd beginning to turn in their direction, and he knew he had to get away at once, regardless of what happened to Allen. He drew back on the reins. Allen turned to him quickly, his gaze startled and searching. McGregor was ready to pull his horse around when the sheriff's towering figure came up beside them. Again McGregor had to wait. He watched the sheriff pass the whip to Allen.

Suddenly the short leather whip was in his own hand, and Allen was leading the stallion again. McGregor didn't remember relinquishing his tight hold of the reins. He was looking at the whip, his nails pressed deep into its leather. He was aware of nothing but the feel of it in his hand. He didn't want the whip, yet he couldn't drop it. He stared at it. Why did he know he should never touch the stallion with it? *Why?*

They were on the track. The stands were a sea of swarming, indistinct faces, strangely quiet while the stallion moved in front of them. Then came a mounting hum of excited voices until suddenly the air was shattered by a continuous roar.

Allen smiled, knowing the crowd was for him and his entry. Night Wind was a Texas thoroughbred, an outsider, while he and his horse *belonged.*

The track announcer said over the public address system, "Coming on the track is Range Boss, owned by the Allen Ranch of Leesburg, Arizona."

The boy felt his blood run hot while the shouts of the crowd rang in his ears. The stallion sidestepped across the track, pulling Allen into a run. McGregor heard himself say to Allen, "Better let go of him now. I'll take him up."

Allen turned the stallion loose, but he remained on the track, sharing his entry's glory. His eyes stayed on the stallion, but his ears were tuned to the voices from the stands, taking in the great acclamation while the black horse moved past. Allen loved every moment of it. Last year it had been this way with Hot Feet. But that had been *after* the race, he reminded himself, when Hot Feet had won the three-year-old crown. This was much too early to feel as he did. His face sobered, and he hurried to catch up to the black stallion.

Going past the stands, the boy held a tight rein. He tried to close his ears to the *familiar,* clamoring cries. He wanted to listen only to the lone beat of hoofs that told him he was free of Allen. Nothing could keep him from leaving now. All he had to do was to take the stallion to the far side of the track and go over the low fence. He'd be on his way before the sheriff or Allen realized what he was doing.

Go now, he told himself savagely. *What are you waiting for?*

The whip was clenched in his hand. He felt his flesh crawl at the touch of it. How long had he been staring at the whip? He turned his eyes away. The stallion snorted and moved faster, hating the tight rein that held him to a slow walk. McGregor rose higher in his stirrups, looking over the small head. He saw the starting gate, stretched halfway across the track. The wire-mesh doors in front were closed. To the right of the gate was a high platform, and standing there was the official starter.

"Hurry that horse!" The starter tried to keep the impatience out of his voice.

All this was so familiar, to McGregor and to the stallion. Couldn't Allen and all the others see that this was no outlaw horse he rode, that he and the stallion had gone to the post before? Even so, what did it matter *now?*

He'd had no intention of going so far, but now he found himself taking his horse around the gate. He felt the mounting tension within him. The stallion shook his head savagely, trying to get more rein. McGregor kept him near the rail and away from the horse who stood just in back of the gate. He turned the stallion's head toward the far turn, yet his own eyes remained on the dark brown horse with white markings on face and legs. He had seen Night Wind before. He was certain of this, too.

He let the stallion lengthen out going away from the gate. He felt reassured of his means of escape in those swift, easy strides. Finally he rose high in his stirrups, and brought the stallion down to a prancing walk. Then he turned him around. He was going back to the gate, even going inside to come out on the break. All the way down the track, he asked himself, *Why?* His only answer was that it didn't matter how they reached the backstretch just as long as they got there. One way around the oval was as good as another. Yet he knew he was lying, that something over which he had no control was taking him and his horse to the starting gate.

The stallion's eyes were on Night Wind. He screamed once and his loud challenge silenced the stands. For a moment every gaze was on him. He came close to the gate, his great black body glistening in the sun, and there was a savage wildness to his action.

One of the starter's assistants walked toward him, and the man's movement broke the stillness of the stands. There came the drone of excited whisperings, for the spectators had caught a glimpse of what they had been told to expect, yet hadn't believed. The Allen Ranch was racing a stallion that had run wild only two weeks ago!

McGregor watched the assistant starter come toward them. He saw the fright in the man's eyes when he reached for the bridle. The stallion reared.

"Get back," McGregor said, bringing his horse down. "I'll take him in alone."

As he moved away, the man said, "Hurry him up then. You got a whip. Use it on him, if you have to!"

Use it on him, if you have to!

The words seemed to tear McGregor's ears apart. He raised the whip before his eyes, staring at it for many seconds. He felt the tears come suddenly, burning his eyelids. Why was he crying? The tears came faster, blinding him. He brushed his hand over them, angrily sweeping them away. He looked toward the stands, searching for the person who had called those very same words to him an eternity ago. The sea of faces swarmed before him. He looked harder, finding Allen, and Larom, and the sheriff on the rail . . . the only faces he knew. He saw a figure suddenly appear behind them, and for a flickering second hope rose within him. Then he recognized Gordon, and turned his attention back to the gate.

At his command, the stallion moved quickly into his starting stall, and the gate closed behind them. There was only one way out now. When the door in front opened there'd be no turning back, *ever.*

He didn't look at the horse and rider in the next stall. His eyes were focused straight ahead and he was looking through the wire mesh at the track that lay before him, so golden in the sun. Suddenly he gasped. And as the air rushed out of his lungs, he knew that here was the true road back that had evaded him for so long, the road that would have told him everything he wanted to know, if he'd found it yesterday or any of the long days before it. Now it wasn't important. Now it was just a means of escape!

The track announcer said, "The horses are at the post." The spectators were quiet, awaiting the start. Their eyes were on the front doors of the gate. They didn't want to miss a thing. They knew that a world of horsepower was ready to explode in a single race. This was to be no usual sprint of three hundred or four hundred yards, but a long mile, twice around the track. This was to be a very special race, and they awaited it in hushed silence.

At the rail near the starting gate, Ralph Herbert removed his horn-rimmed glasses, and quickly wiped the sweat from his eyes. "I don't like this," he told his trainer, a man with a frame as solid and big as his own. "Allen has put something over on us. That black horse isn't fresh off the range. Did you see how he walked into his stall?"

"Yeah, I saw." The trainer worked his jutting square jaw. "But he's wild enough to fight at the drop of a rein. If anything should happen to Night Wind . . ."

"Nothing will happen to him," Herbert said. "But that kid sure can handle that black horse. Look how he's quieting him down, after all his twisting."

"Who is the kid, anyway?"

"Allen said his name's McGregor. Works at the ranch."

"He looks familiar to me," the trainer said, "as I mentioned before."

"Yeah, I know. I'd like to see him without that hat. He's got it pulled far enough down to pretty near cover his eyes."

"And that horse is like something we've seen before, too. He's no mustang, that's for sure. He's bigger than Night Wind and hot-blooded, Ralph."

Herbert said, "I know it. I'm worried. Allen's sprung a race horse on us."

"Maybe so. But there's no doubt that horse has run wild, and done a lot of fighting, Ralph. He's been cut up plenty. Look at his scars."

"I'm still worried."

The trainer smiled. "What for, Ralph? So he's a race horse, and that's why Allen agreed so readily to the mile distance. You think anything here is going to beat Night Wind? Our horse is better than he was last year. You know that as well as I do. If you're going to worry, save it for Santa Anita, when we'll be up against the best again. Even then I won't be worrying, not if Night Wind keeps running the way he's been doing.

Herbert nodded. "I suppose you're right. But just the same I'm glad I have Eddie Malone up on him. I've got ten of my best quarter mares at stake in this race."

"I know that, all right," his trainer answered. "Just don't worry, Ralph."

A short distance down the rail Allen felt a hand from behind grab his arm. He didn't turn. He couldn't take his eyes from the horses in the gate. Any second they'd be off. But Larom and the sheriff turned to the man behind, and Larom said, "Hello, Slim. I didn't think anything would get you this far from Leesburg!"

Allen felt Gordon's fingers digging deeper into his arm, and then Gordon said, "That kid is Alec Ramsay, and the horse is the *Black*. Alec Ramsay and the Black! Did you hear what I said, Allen?" His voice was shrill.

Without turning to him, Allen asked, "You mean McGregor?"

"McGregor nothing. That's not his name. *It's Alec Ramsay!*"

Allen shrugged his shoulders. The kid had the stallion quiet. The break was coming. "What's the difference what his name is, Slim? He's wanted by the police in Salt Lake City. Tom's here to pick him up."

"You're all crazy!" Gordon shouted. "He hasn't done anything! He's Alec Ramsay and the horse is the Black. They're famous, I tell you! Their plane crashed in Wyoming and . . ." The roar of the crowd droned out his words.

"THEY'RE OFF!"

With the opening of the doors, the stallion broke from the boy's restraining hands and came out of the gate in front of Night Wind. McGregor caught a glimpse of the white blaze at his horse's flanks, and then it fell behind quickly as the black stallion's strides steadied and began to lengthen. He drew back on the reins. He called to his horse. He didn't want him running all out. Their race wasn't here, but across the plain! The stretch was short. They'd be at the first turn before he'd be able to pull down the stallion.

Allen's eyes were moist as he pounded Larom on the back. "He'll hold that lead! He's got the race, Hank!" His foreman nodded his head vigorously in complete agreement. Among the thousands who watched, only Herbert and his trainer were silent. They were unimpressed by flying starts from the gate. They knew their champion was built to go a distance and that his speed would mount steadily until he'd run over anything before him.

This was a mile race, and what happened in the first few hundred yards was for fanciers of the quarter horse, and not the thoroughbred. Herbert's clenched hand began pounding the rail, for even now with the horses approaching the first turn Night Wind was gaining!

McGregor slowed the stallion's strides still more. He drew back on the reins, and kept talking to his horse. He heard the fading roar of the crowd as his mount swept into the turn. The stallion's resentment at the tight rein was felt by McGregor in the terrible pull on his arms. The stallion wanted to run and was telling him so forcefully.

"Soon," he called, "but not now!"

He saw the straining, nut-brown body of Night Wind come up on the outside. His jockey was sitting still in the saddle, not asking Night Wind for more speed, but getting it. Their eyes met for a second. The black stallion lowered his head, pulled harder, and picked up speed. The horses reached the middle of the turn, racing stride for stride, stirrup to stirrup.

The boy's head throbbed. He knew Night Wind wasn't going to be taken to the front because that horse couldn't, *wouldn't* run up there. Once in front, Night Wind would relax and start looking around him, forgetting completely about the business at hand unless reminded by his rider.

How did he know this? Why was he so sure of it? Because he remembered seeing Night Wind do just that in the Belmont Stakes. Night Wind had gone into the lead at the half-mile pole. He had stopped then to glance at the far stands. He had been whipped by his jockey and brought on again in the last quarter to win over Hyperion by a head!

McGregor's teeth tore his lips. His memory was coming back! They were entering the backstretch. Here was where they would leave the track. Here was where *his* race would actually begin! He shortened the reins, and the stallion's head came down again. He pulled harder, knowing he would have to fight the stallion to get him off the track.

He saw the look of surprise come to the other rider's face as he succeeded in shortening the stallion's strides, and Night Wind surged ahead. He saw the horse's powerful quarters rise and fall in front of him. He was still watching when Night Wind suddenly relaxed and began to bounce along easily and without effort. Then Night Wind turned his head to the side, interested in the crowd across the infield. His jockey went for the whip, bringing it down solidly on Night Wind's haunches. Once more the whip rose and fell before Night Wind's attention returned to the track ahead, and his strides picked up again.

The boy tried to get the stallion away from the rail and off the track. His fury mounted when the stallion fought him, straining his arms until he could no longer stand the pull. He remembered the whip in his boot and reached for it. Just as he raised it, ready to bring it down, he remembered something else.

A man . . . a short, stocky man standing beside him in the night and wearing only pajamas, his face as white as his disheveled hair . . . a pitchfork in one hand, a whip in the other . . . a raging face and voice saying, "Take the whip. Use it on him if you have to!"

And his own reply in the night, *"If I did, he'd kill me. The same as he would have killed you."*

The whip fell to the track as though he had held a hot coal. His hand seemed to burn, and he placed it on the wet neck before him. Then he leaned forward until his cheek, too, was pressed against his horse. He began talking, sobbing to him. Without realizing what he was doing, he let his hands come up, giving the stallion more rein. He never heard the increased pounding of the lightning hoofs nor was he aware that the backstretch rail was slipping by faster and faster. He was conscious only of the turbulent working of his mind.

The stallion's body and strides were extended until he seemed barely to touch the track. He swept into the back turn, gaining rapidly on the running horse in front of him. Night Wind's jockey glanced back and began using his whip again. But the black stallion's rush was not to be denied. His head was parallel with Night Wind's stirrups as the horses came off the turn and entered the stretch. The crowd was on its feet. Voices shattered the heavens. With still a lap to go, the two horses were racing as one!

Night Wind's jockey rocked in his saddle, using his hands and feet. But he never touched his horse with the whip again, for no longer was it necessary. Night Wind was being challenged, and this was all the champion thoroughbred needed to urge him on to greater speed.

Herbert's fist banged the rail when the horses flashed by him. The kid riding the stallion was making no move. He was sitting absolutely still, almost lifeless, in the saddle, and yet his horse was matching Night Wind stride for stride.

Herbert's trainer said, "Ralph, we got him, I tell you! No horse in the country could get past Night Wind now!"

But the trainer's words provided no solace for Herbert. He had been tricked by Allen. This black horse had raced before. Where had he seen him? Night Wind should have been pulling away from him by now. But he wasn't at all! He was only holding his own.

Not far down the rail, Gordon was screaming at the top of his voice, "Go, Alec! Go!" He pushed between Allen and the sheriff to watch the horses pound into the first turn again.

The sheriff shoved back and said, "Take it easy, Slim. This is just a horse race."

"Just a horse race *nothing!"* Gordon shouted hysterically. "That's Alec Ramsey riding the Black against the fastest thoroughbred in the country! It's the race of the year, and you don't even realize it!"

Allen paid no attention to them. His glazed eyes were on the horses, but they were an indistinct blur to him. "Can anyone see what's happening?" he asked. "Did he get past Night Wind yet?"

"No," Larom answered. "Mac's got a tight hold on him again. He took up rein just after they passed us. That black horse doesn't like it any more than he did before. He's fighting him."

"Why doesn't he let him go?" Allen shouted.

"He's riding. You ask *him,"* Larom said.

McGregor shortened the reins still more, despite the stallion's fury. He pulled him down until Night Wind surged a length ahead and then two lengths more as they came off the turn, entering the backstretch. The boy's mind still erupted with fiery currents that afforded him no peace and produced nothing but a great, flowing mass of conflicting and incoherent elements. Yet sometime within the last few seconds had sprung once more the determination that their race was not to take place here on the track but across the plain. Instinctively he had drawn up on the stallion, trying to force him to respond to his will.

He got his horse away from the rail and to the center of the track, paying no attention to the scarlet-clad jockey on Night Wind, who was drawing farther and farther away from them. His eyes were only for the fighting black head that sought to break his tight hold. He got his horse over closer to the outer rail, working the bit against the corners of the stallion's mouth. His horse fought him more furiously than ever before, and then suddenly bolted back to the center of the track. The boy lost his balance and was thrown forward, his hands grasping the stallion's neck. He felt the great body extend itself again in a determined effort to catch Night Wind. He closed his eyes, sobbing. And then the words came tumbling, bubbling from his mouth, "Black . . . Black . . . Black . . ."

The reins dropped from his hands, his eyes opened, the words kept coming. "Black, I'm Alec Ramsay. I remember. My name is Alec Ramsay. It's come. I know. I know!" Nothing could equal the joy that came to him then. He was free of the darkness. He could remember everything, including his fall from the plane into the treetops, his crashing and tearing through the branches. The details of what had happened after he'd regained consciousness were hazy. But he could remember the groping in the night, the bright headlights, a long ride that had never seemed to end, and then, finally, the desert. Vague though those first hours were to him, he knew that they led directly to Gordon's cottage in the pines, and that he had never been inside a diner, had never taken part in robbery and murder.

All this came to Alec Ramsay in flashing, successive pictures, and then he looked ahead. They were going into the last turn, with Night Wind's lead already reduced to only two lengths! His jockey was swinging his whip back and forth, keeping Night Wind going now that he was running in front all by himself again.

Alec picked up the loose reins. "Go, Black. Go!" he called. Now he was one with his horse. He knew it, and so did the Black! The stallion responded to his call with a new and electrifying burst of speed that sent the earth flying from beneath his hoofs. Gone were the uncertainty and the conflicting wills that had kept them apart for most of the race. No longer did the stallion feel the hard, frenzied pull on his mouth that he had never known before this day. Now he heard the familiar ring of a name that made everything all right again.

"Go, Black. Go!"

Every muscle of the great stallion was strained to its utmost. He came off the turn, drawing alongside the dark, brown champion in great sweeping strides.

The roar of the crowd split Alec's ears, and now it was no different for him here at Preston than it had been at Belmont Park or Churchill Downs. They were in the stretch drive. He strained with his horse, lifting and urging. He hardly breathed. His hat flew off. Night Wind's jockey was riding as if his very life depended upon it. For a few seconds the brown horse matched strides with the Black, and then Night Wind began to fall rapidly behind. His rider turned to Alec, and suddenly recognition came to his eyes when he saw the boy without his hat.

Alec let out a yell. There was nothing more to this race! He remembered all the classic victories he had seen Night Wind win last year, and yet the Black, *who hadn't raced in years,* was running him into the ground! The stallion's strides became ever greater as he swept gloriously down the homestretch. His hoofs pounded with a thunderous rhythm that silenced the voices in the stands. He was a black flame. He was not a horse but a phantom, a flying black shadow in the eyes of the spectators. And they watched him finish the race in quiet homage.

The stands didn't come to life until long after he had left the homestretch. Even then there was no thunderous ovation, only the cries of people asking if what they had witnessed had been seen by others. There were just nods in reply, and none of the spectators took their eyes off the other side of the track where the giant black horse had been brought to a stop. Finally he was turned around and brought back toward them.

* * * * *

 Walter Farley was, without question, the most famous and most read author of books about horses who ever lived.

Horse Sense

Eleanor Bailey

The old doctor and his faithful horse, Judy, had been inseparable for fifteen long years. Judy deserved a rest, and for him, his big chance had finally come. Wonderful news for both of them.

But Judy didn't see it that way.

* * * * *

It was a night when people drew close about their fire and shuddered—not without a pleasurable thrill for their own security—at the thought of those who had to be abroad.

The Allens, way out the River Road, had settled themselves comfortably for the evening. "Dear me!" Mrs. Allen worried as a furious gust of wind drove a sheet of rain against the house, "I hope nobody's out in it." In instant refutation of the hope there came the sound of a horse's hoofs coming down the road, rhythmically pulling out of the sucking mud.

"Aw—the Doctor!" the good lady pronounced in sudden pity. "Going up the ridge to Tulver's." And crossing the room to the window, she ran the blind up quickly to cheer him on his way. And though the lonely wayfarer failed to see the light, something of its message of goodwill and yearning tenderness must have reached him and warmed his heart, for quite suddenly he broke into song—a weird little tune of his own, which though quite off key was yet music to the ears of the splendid chestnut mare he rode. She instantly responded by tucking her head lower against the storm and with new valor settling down for the long, dreary trip that was ahead.

But the song had no chance against the storm. Snatched from the doctor's lips by the jealous wind, drowned in the crash of some forest giant going down before the gale, the tune died out, while on and on the horse and rider went.

* * * * *

It was a marvel how they kept the road, for the night was black and thick. Sometimes the mare stumbled as she came down into an unusually deep rut in the road, but she would catch herself up skillfully and plod bravely on.

"Good girl!" her rider would compliment and reach over and pat her neck; Judy's heart would beat proud at having pleased her master, and with every nerve of her splendid body straining to justify his belief in her, she would throw herself with fresh courage into the task before her.

"Best horse I ever had," the doctor would tell her, as he had told others before her—always believing it, for the doctor had worn out many a good steed in his day. But this one—well, they were growing old together.

"Fifteen years, isn't it, Judy, since I took you in as a partner? That's a long time for a doctor's horse to last. You were the prettiest filly I ever saw," he reminded; "vain as a girl, prancing and bowing your neck. It was love at first sight, wasn't it, eh? You old humbug," as the mare gave an answering toss of her head and a playful shy, "got 'em all faded yet, haven't you, little sweetheart?" Such was the manner of the comradeship between them that had lightened the tedium of many a lonely mile they had traveled together.

It was as they were crossing a bridge over a stream, that the mare stopped suddenly stock still and snorted.

"What is it, Judy?" her rider asked. "Bogey?" And he gave her a gentle urge with his knees. But her only response was a nervous glance around.

"Want me to get down and see?" he interpreted. "All right." And he climbed down and walked ahead.

The water, up to the floor of the bridge, lapped hungrily.

"Whew!" he whistled softly at a sensation of loose, floating boards beneath his feet as he walked on. "This end of it has gone out!" And he gave

a moment's grave consideration to the situation before returning to the horse.

"Can't tell just how much is gone," he reported, quite as if the mare understood. Then he again mounted and explained the situation more fully before urging Judy to proceed.

"Guess we'll have to tackle it, anyhow, Lass," he told her. "It's like this: On the other side of that creek a woman lies at the point of death; tonight, likely, the crisis will come. She's a mother, Judy, the mother of a lot of little children, and mothers can't be spared. It's just up to us to get across someway, I guess."

And gathering up the reins, he gave the gentle urge again. There was no cause to repeat it this time for the mare, though unwilling to proceed on her own initiative, was quite satisfied to accept her master's verdict. Without a moment's hesitancy she went forward onto the loose boards.

There was a second's pause as she came to the end where a section of the bridge had washed away, but it was not the pause of cowardice, but rather of caution—the caution of one who hazards greatly and must choose carefully.

Gropingly, she put a foot forward, then another—and suddenly she had made the plunge into the cold waters! There was an instant's settling as her weight hit the water—a second of suspended action—and then, strong and true, she was swimming toward the bank. It was not far, but the tugging current made every stroke a struggle. Two staunch hearts beat with relief when the bank was reached and climbed.

It was only a couple of miles further, then, to the house of sickness, and when they had reached it a man with a lantern waited anxiously their coming.

"I was afraid maybe you couldn't make it," he said, and the relief in his tone was recompense for the long dangerous trip.

"Oh, Judy and I can make anything," the doctor answered lightly, handing the mare over to the man. "We're a great team, aren't we, partner?" And he rubbed the soft nose that reached out for his caress as he passed.

* * * * *

The winter had passed, summer had come and gone, and now the fall was on the wane. The doctor stood at his office window looking idly down on the street below.

"Another month of this," he ruminated, "and I'll have to store the automobile machine and put the mare in harness again. Poor Judy! This plugging away so steadily year in and year out is beginning to tell on her. She isn't as young as she once was."

It was characteristic of the doctor's self-forgetfulness that though these two conditions fitted him as well as his horse, he did not so apply them. While summer had brought to Judy days of rest and careless freedom in the back lot of the barn, he had plodded along in the same old way—the only difference being that summer complaint, epidemics among the berry-pickers, and accidents with farm machinery had replaced the school contagions and pneumonia of the winter season. And as it was all in the day's work, it did not occur to him to feel sorry for himself at the monotonous grind.

Then, too, even in the hard life of the country doctor, there were compensations. His place in the lives of his people, the love and honor they accorded him; the rides in the open, bringing him close to nature in her tender moods as well as in her tantrums; and more than all, the blessed joy of serving, however humbly—ah, truly the life of the country doctor had its compensations.

And soon, now, it would be winter again!

But the doctor's idle dreaming was broken sharply by a knock at the door. He turned blinking from the light to face the imposing presence of

Oliver K. Trommald, railroad magnate and friend of his college days. For a moment he could not make out who it was that came toward him with outstretched hand and was addressing him in a voice thick with emotion as "Tub Baker, Tub, old man!"

It had been a long time since the doctor had seen Okeh Trommald—two or three times only in the years that stretched back to their college days, so amazingly far, when one stopped to count them—but Trommald's picture was a familiar adornment of the front pages of the papers of the land, and it was this that brought the doctor's recognition and glad greeting.

"Why, Okeh Trommald! Bless my heart! This is good!" And wringing hands and slapping each other on the back and both talking at once like two school-kids, they found seats and settled down to a good old-fashioned visit.

They were a study in contrasts as they sat there, renewing their friendship—the man of big affairs and the country doctor. On the former's well-groomed person there was the unmistakable stamp of his worldly success. One instinctively connected him with handsomely furnished offices where important conferences took place.

As for the doctor, in his shabby setting—the office with its miscellaneous fittings, his shiny clothes that hung so gracelessly on his lean figure—he was the antithesis of the worldly success the other represented. Yet there was a poise in his bearing that permitted him to sit in the presence of the mighty, unabashed—an utter lack of consciousness of his surroundings that seemed to remove him to a plane far above their mediocrity.

Trommald, looking appraisingly about him, found himself marveling at his friend's indifference to what he termed such conspicuous failure. "Lack of success has become a habit with him," was the way he explained it, and he felt a guilty self-reproach for not having extended a helping hand before this.

Poor, old Tub! Well, no more of this struggling obscurity for him, for now Trommald had come to offer him the position of medical director of his railroad lines. It was a plum for which many a big city doctor's mouth had been watering since the death of the incumbent, but Trommald had been saving the place for his old friend.

"What I can't understand," he summed up his mental exploring, with characteristic bluntness, "is how a fellow of your unusual capabilities ever happened to stick in a hole like this. Surely you didn't intend, when you started out, to be a country doctor all your life. Didn't you ever think you'd like to get out and take your rightful place in the world of affairs? Do something worthy of your unusual ability? Not," he added hastily, "that I underestimate your work here. It's splendid and self-sacrificing, I know, but for a man like you, Tub—the honor man of the class—why, your place is with the big men of the country, giving your talents free rein where they'd be appreciated."

* * * * *

The doctor laughed deprecatingly. "You haven't changed, have you, Okeh? Your friends were always big men in your eyes. Just because you have succeeded in a big way you think the rest of us could fill a giant's shoes if we tried."

But Trommald would not be sidetracked by the other's modesty. "I know you could, Tub. What's happened to all those ambitions of your youth? You who were to be a big surgeon at fifty?"

The doctor shook his head, sadly. "Youth is prodigal with its dreams," he sighed. "I guess I've about hit my pace, here."

But his friend would not have it so. "Fiddlesticks!" he dismissed the other's estimate of himself. "Well, I've come to jar you out of your rut." And he stated his mission.

"Don't think I'm being altruistic, either," he ended with the fierceness of one who would hate to be looked upon as a philanthropist. "I'm offering you the place because it's hard to find anyone who just fills the bill, and I happen to know you will."

The doctor was naturally somewhat overcome at the offer. "It's more than I can take in all at once," he said. "I feel like the kid who is used to finding an orange in his stocking who wakes up one Christmas morning to find that Santa Claus has left him his whole pack."

"Well," Trommald settled the matter as he rose to go, "take your time to think it over. I'm going off on a month's hunting trip. I'll be back in time for the directors' meeting the fifteenth. Let me know in time to give them your answer then."

This was mere formality on Trommald's lips. He knew how the other would decide—the only way a man could decide when the main chance offered. The doctor, too, in the innermost recesses of his mind knew what his decision must be. It was too big an opportunity to be passed up, but so momentous a move must receive due consideration.

After his caller had gone, Doc Baker sat for a long time dwelling on this bewildering opportunity that had come his way. Well, well, after all these years! And as he considered, old dreams began to stir within him; forgotten ambitions quickened to life. He suddenly saw himself through the eyes of his successful friend. Sixty-three years old and what had he accomplished? A country doctor plodding along in the drab obscurity in which he had started. He'd be a fool not to accept such an offer. Refusal was not to be thought of. Yet his decision was made and unmade many times before the final burning of his bridges behind him.

* * * * *

It was at the end of a hard day that he sent the telegram to his nephew in the stock country to come and get Judy and take her back with him to end her days in the happy freedom of the range. And when he found his resolution wavering, he turned his mind determinedly to the nagging details of the day just past. He read again the letter of the woman he had pulled through a long siege of illness who was writing to say that she wasn't going to pay him one cent for his services! "I doctored with you for eight months," she wrote, "and got no benefit and then I bought a magic bracelet for twenty five dollars from a professor with spiritual healing in his hands, and after wearing it three days, I was a well woman. So you needn't expect any pay from me." He thought of the family who was vilifying him for enforcing a quarantine and of the child who had died that morning despite his every effort to save it. And suddenly—contrary to his nature, which borrowed no trouble for the future—he found himself thinking with dread of the cold winter to come, his bones shivering in anticipatory chill.

"No, Judy and I have had our last weary ride through the winter's storm and mud. Good old Judy! She certainly has earned her remaining years of rest and ease. And she's going to get them!"

There was no dramatic parting between horse and master when the young nephew came to ride the mare away. The doctor was not given to needless harrowing of his emotions. A few parting instructions as to Judy's care—that was all. Resolutely he turned his mind away from the empty stall, from yearning thoughts of the plucky mare who had traveled the hard road so valiantly with him. When he allowed himself to think of her at all it was to visualize her as galloping in happy freedom over the range of the great stock country, and he found the thought strangely comforting.

* * * * *

The days that were to be the doctor's last in the community he had so faithfully served for forty years were busy ones, indeed. It was no small task to wind up the affairs of years in a few weeks. Then, too, there was a sadness about breaking the peculiar ties that bind a doctor to his people that kept him stirred up and depressed. On every side he met with expressions of tender regard, of honest sorrow at his going, of touching if sometimes ludicrous appeals.

Big Bill Simmons came to him and demanded that before he go he fix up a bottle of medicine that would cure anything any of the Simmonses might get.

"I ain't goin' to have any of these new-fangled doctors doctorin' us," he affirmed.

Mrs. Shumway came to protest at his going. "But, Doctor," she implored, "how *can* we get along without you? Nobody else has ever been able to do anything for us but you. You know that time you were away and we got that Ridgefield doctor for Lutie, and that time Mark was visiting in Seaville and had one of his attacks. I don't know what it is about your treatment," she finished, "but I know *this* much, nobody but you can do *us* any good."

"I'll tell you what it is, my friend," the doctor answered feelingly, "the most powerful curative agency in the potions I mix for you is something you put there yourself—it is your faith in me."

But it was the visit of rusty little Mrs. Brown that tore at his heart strings unbearably. There was something so hopeless about her as she sat there nervously clasping and unclasping her toil-worn hands. The doctor knew so well the tragedy of the years that had bound her to a husband whose violent outbursts of temper bordered on insanity; how courageously her frail person had stood shield between her children and their father's unleashed passion.

"Nobody can handle Jim like you," she declared, "when he's having one of his spells. I couldn't have stood it all these years if it hadn't been for you. Oh, Doctor, don't leave me! *Don't leave me!*"

* * * * *

It was very hard. The farewell reception that his friends gave to him—and to which the whole countryside was asked—was the crowning agony.

"I wish I might be spared these heroics," the doctor grumbled as he got into his best blue serge suit, for he was moved by the touching tribute of his fellow citizens more than he cared to admit.

And if the success of a farewell reception is measured by the regret it expresses, this one was far from a failure. The speeches that tried so hard to be brave and cover with lightness the ache of parting failed so lamentably to do so. As Judge Todd put it: "When you've sort of got used to a fellow standing by in your crises—when he's ushered your little troubles in—and he pinched the ear of the youngest Todd offspring—when he's folded the hands of your loved ones across their breasts, when—well, in short, when he's been to us what our Dr. Baker's been—can we be blamed if the God-speed we ought to give him sticks in our throats?"

The doctor came back to his rooms that night feeling very blue and disheartened. Stripped of his personal effects, the trunk and boxes standing about, the place had a bare, unfamiliar look that was very depressing. Shorn of its personality it seemed to shriek that his tenancy was over, that he was homeless. In vain did he try to tell himself that he would soon be as firmly rooted to another place, that man was but a creature of habit, that once he got used to the new order—

And he would interrupt himself to cry in his heart, *Why, why did I ever let myself be led into this folly? Why, when I was so happy in my sphere, did I listen to the false voice of ambition that has taken away my peace of mind and condemned me to discontent whichever way I turn?* And he would toy with the idea of turning back—Trommald had not yet been apprised of his decision; it was not too late to change his mind. And then with a sigh he would think of Judy, whose sending away had come to represent to him the utter impossibility of turning back. He had given the mare her freedom—freedom she had richly earned—and he was no Indian giver. It was unthinkable that he should call her back from the wide, careless range to face another winter with him. And without Judy—somehow he had not the courage to face the thought of the winter's practice without his faithful ally. And so he fell into troubled slumber.

* * * * *

Judy was in high fettle when she started on her journey. After her long vacation in the lot back of the barn it was good to be on the road again. She expressed her exuberance of spirits in playful shying and skittish pranks that might have made a less expert rider than the doctor's nephew look well to his seating; but young Baker only grinned indulgently. "Take it easy, old girl," he admonished. "You won't feel so snappy after two hundred miles of this."

Indeed, when they had made the stop at a farmhouse for dinner, Judy was glad enough to rest. Experience had taught her the way back was always as long as the way she had come. It would make a good day's traveling for a horse soft from disuse; home would feel mighty good to her that night. But when they had started on after the noon-day rest, it began to penetrate to Judy's consciousness that there was something strange about this trip. Instead of turning back after the stop, according to the routine established by her long association with the doctor, this new rider was taking the road ahead. The mare glanced about nervously, questioning; her gait lagged unwillingly; at every cross-road, she called her rider's attention to his mistake, tactfully suggesting that they turn back here. But it seemed they were going on by intention. When Judy had satisfied herself of this, she accepted the situation gracefully, as became the thoroughbred she was, and devoted her entire energy to getting the trip over as expeditiously as possible.

It was the second day that they began to penetrate that vast, quiet country known to the valley people as "east of the mountains." Great bare hills rose endlessly on every side, casting their shadows on the road that wound through the canyons beside turbulent streams that looked as if they might have their own tales to tell of treachery to the traveler who was caught beside them in the cloudburst season.

Sometimes they passed a ranch house nestling in its clump of poplars in the narrow valley, and a band of stock grazed on the hills. Again and again, Judy neighed greeting when these had proved to be of her own kind, but her voice had only awakened weird echoes that made her flesh creep and filled her with vague uneasiness at the unresponsiveness of the animals she saluted. Were they but phantom creatures, after all, creatures of this strange dream through which she moved?

* * * * *

But her new master explained it more prosaically. "When you've been in this country a while you'll quit wasting your breath hollering to things that look near enough to hear you, but are not," he said. But the experience made Judy more anxious than ever to get this journey over as soon as possible. For it never occurred to her but that at the end of it she would be starting home once more—home to her beloved master and the companionship that made her arduous service with him a joy.

When they had reached their destination and Judy was put in the corral for a day or two to accustom her to her surroundings, she accepted the situation, as she understood it, philosophically. She had reached the end of her journey; a short rest, which she would gladly have foregone to be on the road home, and she would be headed back, away from this country of terrifying sounds, strange scents and sights.

Such a model guest was she in the corral, that on the second day it was decided to turn her out on the range with the other horses. Then it was that terror struck at Judy's heart; a horrible conviction possessed her—they meant for her to stay here always! She began to voice her protest in no uncertain terms.

The doctor's nephew had himself taken her back on the hill and introduced her to the other horses, staying by long enough to see that they accepted her without undue trouble. But when he went to ride back, Judy had followed him down to the lane gate that shut off the range from the barn lot. And when his efforts to drive her back had failed, he was forced to shut the gate in her face and leave her to adjust herself to her new life as best she could.

Bewildered, aghast at the catastrophe that had befallen her, she stood looking across the bars of her exile in stunned inaction. When the import of the man's desertion finally struck her full force, she was like a thing possessed. Frantically she tore up and down the fence looking for an opening, stopping now and then, her eyes wild with terror, to look over the bars toward man's habitation—a place she had never before looked in vain for help—while her neigh rang out incessantly, mad with longing.

"That girl you brought up from down below has got a mighty purty voice, Bake," one of the range hands twitted the doctor's nephew at dinner.

"Say, what's the matter with her anyway," another wanted to know. "Never made no fuss at all the first two days, and just listen to her now!"

"I insulted her, taking her for a horse and trying to make her associate with the other horses on the range. She's used to being treated like one of the family," young Baker informed them. "Oh, well," he dismissed the matter comfortably, "she'll get over it by night."

* * * * *

But such was not the case. For three days and nights Judy ceaselessly tore up and down the fence that imprisoned her, sending her homesick cry out at regular intervals. In the daytime it did not so much matter, but her abuse of the night began to get on everyone's nerves.

"Talk about the coyotes' serenade! That pack of 'em that was quarreling over the carcass of a dead calf outside the bunkhouse a couple of weeks ago was regular pikers compared to this here!" someone put it.

The fourth day brought no change in Judy's condition, but abruptly that night her frantic neighing ceased, her restless hoofbeats were still, as quietly calculating she stood before the high fence that imprisoned her.

It *was* a high fence; previous investigation had told her it was madness for her to try to jump it. But she had reached that stage of desperation where her home hunger outweighed all else. If she died in the attempt, she must make it.

Still as an equestrian statue she stood revealed in the moonlight—taut, calculating, every force of that splendid body gathering for the supreme effort. She made several little tentative runs forward before she could whip her courage up sufficiently to dare the final trial. And then, like a streak, she was shooting forth, crouching for the spring, lifting herself with an apparent ease that suggested some huge-winged bird rising for flight.

It was unfortunate that there was none but the full moon to see the beauty of the technique of that hurdle, developed in an hour of need, the magnificent form with which the riderless horse swung out glad and free on her way home.

At the breakfast-table that morning, Judy was once more the subject of conversation. "Well, the old mare finally wore herself out and decided to join the other horses, I guess," someone hazarded. "Honest, she'd kept up her fretting so long that when it stopped, the quiet woke me up."

"Me, too," another affirmed. But nobody had roused sufficiently to hear Judy's galloping footsteps go down the road toward home.

* * * * *

Like a thing pursued, she traveled, scarcely stopping to eat or rest. Her hoofbeats roused the quiet canyons to unfamiliar echoes, but save for an occasional rancher, there was none to hear and wonder. It was a lonely way—the hills that looked so sinister when the shadows of night were on them, the canyons that were dark and gloomy even at noonday, but these things aroused no fear in Judy's heart, now. She beheld them as the traveler from his comfortable Pullman beholds the homestead on the desolate prairie. Even when in the eerie hours of the morning a coyote crossed her path with a magpie in its mouth, she gave it but a passing glance. She was bound for home!

It was the second night that she came to the toll bridge over Swift River. The gate was closed; but Judy's indomitable spirit knew no faltering now. With scarcely a moment's pause she turned aside and went down the bank.

The keeper, aroused from his sleep by the sound of the rolling rock and the plunging body, sat up in frozen horror. "Oh!" he said as he jumped out of bed, "someone's trying to ford the river!" But when he had reached the bank to offer what aid he could, to his amazement he saw a riderless horse scramble up the opposite bank and gallop off.

* * * * *

The doctor's dreams were troubled that night. Unprepared, he stood before a gathering of learned men trying to make his speech, but to his great embarrassment he could think of nothing to say. He was running for a train, and his feet kept going up and down in the same place. The stable was on fire, and when he went to lead Judy out she was nowhere to be found. Frantically he was searching for her, when suddenly he heard her neigh outside. A great weight lifted from his mind. She was there safe. A sense of well-being pervaded his soul as he awoke from the dream, but it vanished quickly as his eyes beheld the disordered room—the books and pictures piled about, the trunk and packing boxes. Like clogs slipping into place his troubles found him.

Suddenly he sat up in bed and listened, with the air of one sure that his ears had tricked him! The imperious summons sounded again! With a bound he was at the window, then flying into his clothes.

It was Judy neighing to be let in!

Just what passed between horse and master as they met after their separation is a matter of conjecture. Like as not, Judy nosed the doctor's shoulder and nibbled at his coat sleeve, while he slapped her sweaty, dusty neck and chided her fondly somewhat in this manner:

"You old humbug! Haven't you got sense enough to know when you're well off? Send you off to spend the rest of your days in horse paradise, and here you are back begging to be put to work again. Well, nothing for it, I guess, but do as you say. No cure for that ailment, far as I know. Got it myself. 'Rutitis,' it's called. Get in a rut and can't get out—don't want to get out. Just want to stay there till you die. Happy death, though. Whoopee! Judy, I'll wire Trommald that I can't come!"

* * * * *

"Horse Sense," by Eleanor Bailey. Published February 18, 1922, in the Christian Herald. *Reprinted by permission of Christian Herald, Inc. Eleanor Bailey wrote for inspirational magazines during the first half of the twentieth century.*

The Thinking Horses of Elberfeld

Maurice Maeterlinck
Commentary by Francis H. Rowley

Of all the subjects and books we study, we know perhaps least about the natural world—the inner world of the birds, insects, fish, reptiles, and animals with whom we share this planet.

We laughingly put them down with the double pun "dumb animals," implying that they are both stupid and incapable of producing sound, whereas they are neither.

One of the greatest minds to come out of the nineteenth century was that of Nobel Prize–winning dramatist, philosopher, naturalist, and poet, Maurice Maeterlinck (1862–1949).

* * * * *

In Elberfeld, Germany, there is a prosperous manufacturer, Herr Krall, who owns, among other horses, a Shetland pony, Haenschen, and two Arabian stallions, Muhamed and Zarif. These horses, by feats of what is apparently extraordinary mental skill, have attracted the attention of learned men from celebrated universities and elsewhere who have visited them and studied them. They have been taught an alphabet in which each letter is designated by a certain number of blows struck by the right foot and the left foot. The answers to mathematical problems are given by them in the same way—that is, by certain blows of the feet. Their owner, who has surrounded them with an atmosphere of affection that has, in a manner of speaking, humanized them, says of Muhamed: "Within a fortnight of the first lesson he did simple little addition and subtraction sums quite correctly. He had learned to distinguish the tens from the units, striking the latter with his right foot and the former with his left. He knew the meaning of the symbols plus and minus. Four days later he was beginning multiplication and division. In four months' time he knew how to extract square and cubic roots, and, soon after, he learned to spell and read by means of the conventional alphabet."

Dr. E. Clarapède, of the University of Geneva, is quoted, after making a study of these horses, as pronouncing the phenomenon "the most sensational event that has ever happened in the psychological world."

* * * * *

The master, standing beside the blackboard, chalk, in hand, introduces me to Muhamed in due form, as to a human being: "Muhamed, attention! This is your uncle"—pointing to me—"who has come a long way to honor you with a visit. Mind you don't disappoint him. His name is Maeterlinck." Krall pronounces the first syllable German fashion, *mah.* "Do you understand—Maeterlinck? Now show him you know your letters and that you can spell correctly, like a sensible child. Go ahead, we're listening."

Muhamed gives a short neigh and on the small, movable board at his feet strikes first with his right hoof, and then with his left, the number of blows which correspond with the letter M in the conventional alphabet used by the horses. Then, one after the other, without stopping or hesitating, he marks the letters A D R L I N S H, representing the unexpected aspect which my humble name assumes in the equine mind and phonetics. His attention is called to the fact that there is a mistake. He readily agrees, and replaces the "S H" by a "G," and then the "G" by a "K." We insist that he must put a "T" instead of the "D," but Muhamed, content with his work, shakes his head to say no and refuses to make any further corrections.

I assure you that the first shock is rather disturbing, however much one expects it. I am quite aware that when one describes these things, one is taken for a dupe too readily dazzled by the doubtless childish illusion of an ingeniously contrived scene.

Lest it might be thought that the answers given were dependent upon the presence of the owner and certain signs from him, the owner leaves Maeterlinck alone with the horses, saying "Try it for yourself. Dictate to the horses any German word of two or three syllables, emphasizing it strongly. I shall go out of the stable and leave you alone with him."

* * * * *

Behold Muhamed and me by ourselves. I confess that I am a little frightened. I have many a time felt less uncomfortable in the presence of the great ones or the kings of the earth. Who am I dealing with exactly? However, I summon my courage and speak aloud the first word that comes to me, the name of the hotel at which I am staying: Weidenhof. At first, Muhamed seems a little puzzled by his master's absence, appears not to hear me, and does not even deign to notice that I am there. But I repeat eagerly, in varying tones of voice, by turns insinuating, threatening, beseeching, and commanding: "Weidenhof! Weidenhof! Weidenhof!"

At last my mysterious companion suddenly makes up his mind to lend me his ears and straightaway blithely raps out the following letters, which I write down on the blackboard as they come: "W-E-I-D-N-H-O-Z." It is a magnificent specimen of equine spelling!

* * * * *

More remarkable perhaps than the answers in names spelled out by these horses is the facility and quickness with which they answer mathematical problems. Krall asks me for two numbers to multiply. I give him 63 times 7. He does the sum, and writes the product on the board, followed by the sign of division: 441 ÷ 7. Instantly, Haenschen, with a celerity difficult to follow, gives three blows, or rather, three violent scrapes, with his right hoof, and six with his left, which makes 63, for we must not forget that in German they say, not "sixty-three," but "three and sixty." We congratulate him, and, to evince his satisfaction, he nimbly reverses the number by marking 36, and then puts it right again by scraping 63.

What shall we think, for example, of a horse that, asked to give the square root of 4,096, replies at once, 64?

But probably to many of us the most astonishing thing that Herr Krall reports is that upon two different occasions on his return from a business trip, one of these horses spelled out to him information of things that had happened in his absence.

"One morning, for instance, I came to the stable, and was preparing to give him his lesson in arithmetic. He was no sooner in front of the spring-board than he began to stamp with his foot. I left him alone, and was astounded to hear a whole sentence, an absolutely human sentence, come letter by letter from his hoof: 'Albert has beaten Haenschen;' was what he said to me that day. Another time I wrote down from his dictation: 'Haenschen has bitten Kama.' "

Krall, for that matter, living in the midst of his miracle, seems to think this quite natural and almost inevitable. I, who have been immersed in it only a few hours, accept it almost as calmly as he does. I believe without hesitation what he tells me, and in the presence of this phenomenon which, for the first time in man's existence, gives us a sentence that has not sprung from a human brain, I ask myself whither we are tending, where we stand, and what lies ahead of us.

* * * * *

Must we once more repeat, in connection with these startling performances, that those who speak of audible or visible signals, of telegraphy, of expedients, trickery, or deceit are speaking of what they have not seen? There is but one reply to be made to anyone who honestly refuses to believe:

Go to Elberfeld—the problem is sufficiently important, sufficiently big with consequences, to make the journey worthwhile—and, behind closed doors, alone with the horse, in the absolute solitude and silence of the stable, set Muhamed to extract a half a dozen roots, which like that which I have mentioned, require so many operations. You must yourself be ignorant of the solutions so as to do away with any transmission of unconscious thought. If he then gives you, one after the other, five or six correct solutions, as he did to me and many others, you will not go away with the conviction that the animal is able by its intelligence to extract those roots, because that conviction would upset too thoroughly the greater part of the certainties on which your life is based. But you will, at any rate, be persuaded that you have been in the presence of one of the greatest and strangest riddles that can disturb the mind of man, and it is always a good, salutary thing to come into contact with emotions of this order.

An unexpected breach is thus made in the wall behind which lie heaped the great secrets which seem to us, as our knowledge and our civilization increase, to become stranger and more inaccessible. True, it is a narrow breach; but it is the first that has been opened in that part of the hitherto uncrannied wall which is not turned toward mankind. What will issue through it? No one can foretell what we may hope.

* * * * *

"The Thinking Horses," by Maurice Maeterlinck. Published October 27, 1914, in The Youth's Instructor. *Reprinted by permission of Joe Wheeler (P.O. Box 1246, Conifer, Colorado 80433) and Review and Herald® Publishing Association, Hagerstown, Maryland. Maurice Maeterlinck (1862–1949) Belgian poet, dramatist, and essayist, was awarded the Nobel Prize for literature in 1911.*

The Timid-Brave

Aline Havard

The wild Montana country was still new to this sixteen-year-old eastern tenderfoot. Yet, new or not, with her brother's condition, if help didn't come soon—very soon!. . .

Redskin represented her only hope.

* * * * *

Ellen Graham stood at the ranch-house door watching the sun drop behind the snowy heights of Mount Blackfoot and spread its golden rays for an instant over the prairie valley. She caught her breath in a quick, involuntary sigh. It was beautiful, and she loved it—this Montana upland, this lonely, mountain-girded valley which had been her home for a year, ever since the New York doctor had sent her father west, had ordered him to give up city life for cattle farming. But though Ellen loved the Blackfoot valley, she was not quite enough at home in it, not self-reliant enough by nature, to feel happy at being left alone for three days with Don, her twelve-year-old brother, and Eliza, the housekeeper. And now she had a letter in her hand that announced that another two days must pass before her father's return. The business, which had called him to Omaha, prolonged his absence. Ellen knew she had nothing to fear, even with the cowboys off on the range and the ranch left alone. Yet it was hard to feel resigned and to speak cheerfully to the boy who now came running toward her from around the house.

"Don, Father's not coming home till Saturday. And here's a letter he wants taken to Mark Jackson. It's about paying the herders, I think. I'd rather you'd get Joe to ride over with it. The sun's going down."

Don took the letter from his sister's hand. Though she had stood in a mother's place to him for ten years, still he did not obey her very readily nor feel her sixteen years were much more than his own twelve. He had an alert, merry face, beneath thick brown hair. Ellen's blond slenderness, her soft blue eyes and sweetness of expression made her seem almost childish beside the strong, resolute boy. He treated her with a kind of affectionate tolerance.

"Nobody's 'round," he said. "Joe's out on the range. I'll saddle Buff and take it myself. He's a good mount. Don't worry, Sis. I'll be back soon."

Without waiting for comment, he ran toward the stables grouped behind the ranch house, caught a sorrel pony from the paddock, and put on saddle and bridle. Westward, the sky was streaked with brilliant colors. The mountainsides held silver and violet shadows. The springtime air in the valley was cool and pure to breathe. But the boy tightening the pony's girths noticed none of this. Don's eyes lighted on a revolver which had been thrust into the saddle holster by the last cowboy rider. He whistled, swung himself onto Buff's back with a little thrill of pleasure at the feel of the pony between his knees and the look of the revolver beside him, and passing the gate, trotted eastward across the valley to the mountains.

The trail to Jackson's ran through a shallow canyon at the foot of Eagle Butte, a low peak crowning the eastern range of hills, five miles across the valley from Mount Blackfoot's towering heights.

After leaving the level openness of the valley, Buff entered a ravine, followed a rough path checkered by late rays of sunlight shining through the leaves, and presently drew up of his own accord before the lonely little wooden house of the cattleman. Don dismounted and ran to the door. It was opened by a boy of his own age with a tanned and freckled face and a shock of red hair.

"Hello, Don!" he said, grinning. "A letter for Dad? He's out on the range, but I'll put it on the mantel shelf for him. You going right home?"

"I ought to. It's getting late," said Don. "Markie, can you shoot?"

"Sure," said the other, easily. "Oh, you got a gun? Let's see." He pulled the revolver from Buff's saddle holster.

"It's not mine. I can't shoot much," Don admitted. "But I'd like to try."

"Let's try now. I'll teach you. Come back in the woods. Trees make a good target. Why, it's hardly sunset. You'll be home in plenty of time."

Don surrendered. The sunlight still looked golden. He followed his friend into the woods. Here the lesson in shooting went on with keen interest as long as the cartridges lasted. Don missed all his shots, and Markie, having made two hits, jeered at him. When at last Don mounted Buff and took the homeward road, the sun had vanished, and in the canyon, trees and shrubs were but vague outlines, black shadows bordering the rocky and difficult slope.

Buff's restless trot perforce slackened to a walk as he picked an unwilling way through the darkness. His rider, uneasy too, urged him on with a false air of confidence. Suddenly the pony stopped short, staring at the branch of a tree which overhung the path. Buff was shaking all over with fear. "Go on, Buff! Go on!" whispered Don, trembling too. Don's eyes were now fixed upon the branch. Something dark hung there, something that was not the young leafy clusters, and all at once two yellow eyes gleamed out like flames. The body moved, its lithe shape crept nearer. The pony gave one bound of terror, reared sharply, plunged forward, flung his rider headlong to the ground, and galloped away.

The clatter of his flying hoofs did not reach Don's ears. He fell on a sharp ledge of stone; one of his ribs snapped with a jagged pain, and he lost consciousness. The mountain lion crept down from the tree and sniffed at him. The boy lay as if dead, and the lion, having dined well off a fat calf stolen from the herd, left him there and slunk off into the shadows.

The early northern darkness had fallen when Ellen, with old Eliza's help, saddled her pony and started out to look for Don. Used to the casual and irregular habits of the cowboys, she dared not wait for Joe's return from the range. Alone, by the starlight's first faint gleam, she rode eastward toward Eagle Butte, anxiety for Don almost conquering her instinctive fear of darkness and solitude. She had not ridden a mile when she heard the sound of hoofs drawing near. Buff was advancing at a restless walk—with Don huddled on his back.

"Don! What's wrong? Are you hurt?" gasped his sister. She laid hold of Buff's bridle rein, for the boy had not answered nor even raised his head. All his strength was spent in keeping Buff from breaking into a trot.

Not until the ranch house was reached could he whisper to Ellen something of what had befallen him—of how he had recovered his senses, had struggled to his feet, and driven on by fear of the lion, had found Buff wandering a hundred yards ahead, not quite willing to desert his master, and had managed to mount him and ride toward home. Don's head was burning with fever; his mind wavered between truth and fancy; his broken rib and bruised body tormented him. When Ellen and Eliza had put him to bed he fell into delirium, clutched at his aching breast and cried out to be saved from the lion's claws. Ellen sat with a white face by his bedside, watched his gasping breath, and thought that he grew worse with every passing moment.

It was an hour later when Eliza found her in the hall, wearing a sheepskin jacket, a round woolen cap pulled over her fair hair, and her riding breeches thrust into leather boots of Don's which buckled close about the knee. "Where are my gloves, Eliza? I can't think," she stammered.

"Why . . . why . . . they're here, but where are you going, Miss Ellen?" asked the housekeeper, amazed.

"I've got to go! Joe's not back. Don's dying!" Ellen choked down a sob.

The kindhearted, reasonable old woman broke in, "No, he's not. But go where? Where can you go?"

"For the doctor who's been here to see Father—for Dr. Digby at the Indian reservation. . . ."

"At the Agency! Across Mount Blackfoot!"

"Yes. I'm going there. Don't argue with me. Do you think I can sit here and see Don die?"

"You, Miss Ellen! You cross the mountain at night?" Aghast, Eliza stared at the girl's childish figure, at her blue eyes shining with pain and terror, at her trembling hands which fumbled with the gloves. But without waiting to answer, Ellen ran from the house and toward the paddock, to the fence of which was tied her bay pony, Redskin, not yet unsaddled after her ride in search of Don.

There was no use in stopping to tell Eliza she was not afraid. Ellen was not actress enough to deceive anybody. She was afraid with every bit of her mind and every nerve in her body—so afraid that the very shadows of house and fences made her start and shudder. The moon, three-quarters full, was just rising over Eagle Butte. Its pale light touched the frosty heights of Mount Blackfoot as Ellen's fearful eyes turned westward to look at the mountain across which her path lay. How different it looked now from in the summer days soon after their arrival in the valley when she and Don had ridden the mountain trail with neighbors from the lower ranches, with Markie Jackson and his father. Even then they had gone no higher than the timberline. They had not climbed to the snowfields, much less descended the peak's far side to the level of the Indian Agency.

The cold April air stung her cheeks as she urged Redskin through the paddock gate and out across the valley. She spoke softly to the reluctant pony, patting his warm neck. All her hope was in the sturdy little beast she rode. For Redskin's old home was the reservation. Mr. Graham had bought him from Dr. Digby, the resident physician, who for years had ridden him over the mountain trail. That lonely road was the path Redskin knew best. It was this knowledge which had helped Ellen to conquer her fear enough to attempt the night ride. For her brother's sake, she could face the unknown terrors which lay ahead, but she knew that her frightened, whirling brain would never be able to search out the trail. This she must leave to Redskin, hoping only to keep sense and courage enough to cling to his back and bear her message to Dr. Digby's door.

Though the mountainside was in black shadow, the trail was clearly visible in the moonlight as it wound upward from the valley. At first, Ellen recognized its landmarks—a jutting oak, a pile of rocks, or a bit of grassy open. The gentle slope grew steeper as the valley was left behind. With bent head and straining shoulders, Redskin climbed steadily on through scattered groves of pine and cedar, across grass-dotted clearings, up toward the forests on the mountain's flank. With every hundred yards the air grew colder. Another mile, and the moonlit trail ended. Ellen drew rein and stared into the dense shadows of the close-growing pines, her knees shaking.

"I can't go on, Redskin! I'm afraid!" she whispered.

The pony turned his head inquiringly. Impatient to finish his task, his pawing hoofs echoed sharply through the silence. Ellen loosed the rein, and pony and rider were swallowed up in the forest darkness.

The pines murmured through the fragrant gloom. Redskin's hoofs thudded crisply on the pine-needle carpet. But his hoof beats seemed repeated and multiplied in the darkness beyond the trail. All around her

Ellen heard footsteps, whispers, hurried breathing. The forest was alive with—what? With bears, whose home it was? Dr. Digby had told her father of bear hunts on moonlit nights along the mountainside. Were bears snuffing their trail now, or were the indistinct noises filling her ears no more than the whisper of the pines and the rustle of the needles under the pony's feet? Already Ellen was long past knowing that this was more likely the truth. Terror had crept with an icy touch along her spine. Her heart leaped and hammered in her breast; her hand shook on the rein; and through chattering teeth she whispered, "Go on, Redskin! You know the way. I'm afraid!"

Up and up they climbed, until the pine trees thinned to scattered groves, the air grew piercingly cold, and snow sifted here and there along the ground. The bleak wind from the mountain peak was as cold as the snowfields it had passed over. The tall trees changed to dwarfish, storm-tossed shrubs. Redskin shook his head, but doggedly climbed on. The cold swept against Ellen's face, stiffened her cheeks and hands, and robbed her of the last cherished remnants of courage. She wept in silent misery, and the icy wind dried her tears before they fell.

The last wind-beaten shrub was left behind. Before them spread the wide desolation of the snowfields girdling the peak of Mount Blackfoot—that white, glittering peak wreathed in snow streamers which made such a glorious sight to look at from the valley's shelter. Ellen gathered up the reins in her stiffened hands. One misstep on the snow-covered, treacherous trail might plunge pony and rider down hidden ravine or rocky slope. She stared ahead over the moonlight-flooded waste, at ice-clad rocks and snow drifts bounding the frozen, slippery path. The stars shone brightly now, and the moon was high, but the powdery snow, whirled on the fierce blast, danced through the air like a misty curtain. Its hard particles struck Ellen's face and lips as, hopeless of guiding Redskin up the trail, she stammered into the ear cocked back from the pony's toiling head, "I don't know the way, Redskin! But you do. Oh, please do! Keep on the trail, Redskin, keep on the trail! That's our only chance!"

They seemed hung now between earth and heaven. Below them, the gloom of the forest; above, the moon and stars in the deep blue sky. Around them was a white wilderness of bitter cold, an icy wind that chilled the blood, that drove the breath from Ellen's numbed and shuddering body until she swayed in the saddle.

Her mind began to fail. She found herself muttering nonsense in Redskin's ear and calling on him for help and encouragement. But in the back of her head remained the steadfast thought: *Never mind what I say. It's just because I'm afraid. If we can get on. . . .* Yet the time came when she was so numb with cold she dreaded to fall from the pony's back and lie freezing to death in the snow. She dared not dismount to restore some motion of blood to her limbs, for she had not strength left to mount again, to scramble to the pony's back from that narrow, slippery path bounding the snow-masked cliffs. By moments the thought returned to her of Don lying in the ranch house, fever-flushed, groaning with pain, and then she shook the reins and spoke with desperate pleading, "Go on, Redskin!"

But the wise pony would not be urged to speed on such a trail as this. He toiled up another slope, rounded a frozen promontory, and paused, panting, on a shelving verge below which the snowfields of Mount Blackfoot's farther side dropped again to timberline. Below that, the black shadow of the forest recommenced. It had all to be lived through once more—the horror-haunted journey!

Ellen raised stiff, aching arms and pulled her woolen cap down over her head. Her blond hair, tossed by the keen wind, wound itself about her face and neck. She had neither breath nor courage to speak, but she touched Redskin's shoulder. He gave a great sigh of weariness and began the perilous descent.

When the hands and feet are numb, the mind dazed and foggy, one can get pretty near to freezing without knowing it. Ellen was so stiff in the saddle, her face so flayed by the cold wind, her thoughts so slow and dull, she hardly suffered at all as Redskin picked his dangerous way down through the snow on the western flank of Mount Blackfoot. She first realized her own condition by feeling a sudden rush of warmth and darkness as the pony left the moonlight snow to enter the forest. With smarting eyes, she stared about her, breathing the fragrant, pine-laden air. The world of snow was left behind. Evergreens stirred and sighed around her. The moonlight was dimmed to a pale, checkered radiance. But with the sudden rise in temperature, long shudders caught her spine, her numbed hands and feet began to throb with pain. For a time, this pain kept her slow thoughts fixed upon it. She writhed in the saddle, vainly seeking relief. It was not until her head somewhat cleared and her mind worked quicker that she became aware of noises in the forest near her, of a breaking twig and the swish of pine needles under what sounded like a cautious tread. Redskin sniffed uneasily, pricking his ears.

The daze of cold left Ellen's mind, driven out by a return of terror, of the old wearing, weakening fear which had shaken her throughout the night journey. "What is it, Redskin?" she stammered. The pony tossed his head, his ear still cocked. In the forest to the right of the trail the sounds increased, developed into a light, occasional step, and the slow passage of a body between low-hanging evergreen boughs. This time it was no phantom of Ellen's vivid fancy. Something was approaching the trail—not directly, but in hiding, creeping along beside it, watching from behind the green branches. Ellen's eyes were fixed on the shadowy outlines of the forest trees which pressed close upon the trail. She was too paralyzed with fear to notice that the pony was not afraid, that his cocked ear and sniffing nose showed no more than eager curiosity. She was beyond reasoning. A twig broke beneath the intruder's step. There was but one image in Ellen's mind as, blank and helpless, she watched for whatever should break from cover before her eyes. She thought a mountain lion was tracking her, waiting for the best chance to spring upon its prey. The green branches parted; something looked out into the pale, glimmering moonlight—a furry head above bright dark eyes. Ellen's heart leaped from its place as the world reeled into blackness before her. She fell senseless on Redskin's neck, at which the pony stopped short and looked back for guidance to the Indian, who, dragging his rifle after him, ran to Redskin's side.

* * * * *

It was more than an hour later when Dr. Digby was roused from sleep by vigorous knocking at his door. Hurrying out, he found an Indian standing beside a pony and holding something on its back.

"Is that you, Flying Eagle? What have you there?" demanded the doctor.

The Indian burst into speech: "Flying Eagle make the night hunt on the mountain. He hear pony's feet coming down from snow heights. He watch and listen and soon see Redskin, pony doctor sell Mr. Graham in Blackfoot valley. And on pony's back little white squaw belong daughter Mr. Graham. Little squaw feel too much cold and fear. She fall asleep. I bring her here."

The two men carried Ellen into the house. The warmth and the movement roused her one moment from her lethargy. The thought so long present in her bewildered mind forced itself to her lips as the doctor's familiar face bent over her. "Doctor! Go to him—to Don! He's hurt!"

"So that's it. Lay her down here." Ellen heard no more than this as she sank again into unconsciousness.

It was bright morning and the room was full of sunlight when she opened her eyes and stretched her sore, aching body. For an instant the feeling of comfortable warmth was so delicious, she could think of nothing else. But the next, she started up, gasping, as memory flooded back. She had tried to reach the Agency. Was she there? Had she given her message? The room was unfamiliar. She heard the sound of horses' hoofs, and raised herself on stiff arms to look from the window. But before she had succeeded, the door was softly opened, and Dr. and Mrs. Digby entered, with Flying Eagle at their heels. The doctor wore riding clothes, and his boots were wet with snow. He pulled off his gloves and flicked his cold hands together.

"Did you go to him, doctor?" Ellen cried out, her shoulders trembling as she tried to pull herself upright in bed.

The doctor sat down beside her and pushed her back against the pillows. "We've just returned from the valley," he said. "Take that frightened look off your face, child. Don is all right. He's a sick boy, but I left him well bandaged and fairly comfortable. And I left Eliza more comfortable, too, when she heard you were here." The doctor's kind, bright eyes kept themselves fixed upon Ellen's face, grown peaceful and happy, and there was wonder in his quiet voice as he went on: "It took us—Flying Eagle and myself—a good while to cross the mountain. There was a strong wind blowing all night, and the trail is bad. How you ever . . ." He stopped and caught Ellen's hand in his.

The Indian had pushed curiously forward and was staring at Ellen with intense interest. Now he gave a slow shake of the head. "Yes, very bad, doctor," he echoed. "Very bad trail at night for men. Yet this little pale squaw she make it all alone—the Timid-Brave."

* * * * *

"The Timid Brave," by Aline Havard. Published August 1924 in St. Nicholas. *Text owned by Joe Wheeler. Aline Havard wrote for popular magazines during the first half of the twentieth century.*

Good Sale

Caroline Young

For two years they had boarded Pinto, but now the owner was coming back to reclaim him. Montie was devastated, for Pinto was the only horse she loved.

Later, there came the opportunity to sell some rather wild horses. Her father being gone, she could make the sale, and buy Pinto back.

But, to her chagrin, the ethics of her father kept her from making the sale.

* * * * *

Montie stared with incredulous eyes at the letter her father handed her. She folded the single sheet at last and shook her head.

"He's coming to get Pinto! It just doesn't seem possible, Father, that I have to give up Pinto. Why, it's . . . it's just like I owned him! I've had him so long!"

"But Pinto's never been really yours, Montie," protested Mr. Searles. "You've known that you'd have to turn him over to his owner some day."

"Yes, but . . . "

Montie whirled suddenly and disappeared into the house. She could not trust herself to speak further just then. Of course, she tried to reason as she lay face down on her cot, Pinto wasn't hers—never had been. His owner had left him with her father to board for a very nominal sum, with the understanding that Montie and her father might ride him all they wished.

Two years had passed since Mr. Jordan had gone back East. Business and a long illness had delayed his return to his western interests, the letter said, but now he was coming—would be there any day. And he would take Pinto away from her!

There were always other horses on the Searles's place; but now as Montie called them before her in mental review, there wasn't one that could take Pinto's place. There wasn't a really good horse in the lot. No gentle, trustworthy mount like hers. She shuddered as she thought of Rox and Nell, the handsomest ones. They were vicious, for all their black sleekness. Mose was not vicious, but he was impossibly slow. And so on, down the line. There wasn't one to take Pinto's place. Anyway, Pinto was—well, just Pinto. Even had there been another pony equally swift, equally gentle, equally handsome, he wouldn't have been her beloved Pinto!

It was after supper when Mr. Searles was reading the letter again, that Montie spoke to him of a plan she had been revolving in her mind the last few hours.

"Father, couldn't we buy Pinto? Mr. Jordan ought to be willing to sell him. He hasn't seen him for a long time, and he didn't ride him much when he was here. He isn't attached to him."

Her father looked at her over his spectacles. "I wish I could buy him for you, Montie, but there's no use thinking about it. The horse trading business isn't what it once was. There's barely enough money in it to keep us going here. There's nothing left with which to buy horses outright. There'll always be horses to use," he finished in an apologetic tone.

"I wonder . . ." began Montie in a hesitant voice, "I wonder if Joe Elkins wouldn't buy Rox and Nell. He surely liked their looks. Said they'd make a pretty team."

"You know why I wouldn't sell that team to Joe. His mother will have to drive his team once in a while. I'm not deceiving anybody when it comes to horses. Or anything else, for that matter."

"Maybe Joe could tame them down," suggested Montie.

"I intend to sell those horses to someone who knows horseflesh. Someone who can handle them right. Joe means well, but he can't manage a fractious horse. 'Twouldn't be decent for me to sell him Rox and Nell. You know that, Montie."

"But it may be months before anyone else who wants to buy them comes along," protested Montie. "By that time Pinto will be gone."

"I'm sorry about Pinto," said Mr. Searles. "Mighty sorry. But you'd better go to bed now and forget your troubles. Don't forget, though, that your daddy has never knowingly deceived anyone about a horse."

* * * * *

Montie was awakened early next morning by the labored chug-chug of a motor striving to make the grade from the bridge over Crystal Creek up the hill atop of which she lived. Running to her window, she peered out. There was no mistaking the portly gentleman who sat beside Joe Elkins in his little roadster.

She had hoped that Mr. Jordan wouldn't come for a few days, but here he was, close on the heels of his letter. Joe, even as he drove, was gazing toward the corral as if to see whether the team he coveted was still there.

Montie dressed with lightning speed and rushed out to join the little group at the gate. Her father had already brought Pinto up when she reached the spot.

"Well, your father tells me you've had a nice time riding my horse," said Mr. Jordan, shaking hands with her in his hearty way. "I expect you'll hate to see him go, but it looks as if you'd still have plenty of horses to ride."

Beyond the fence, Nell tossed her mane and snorted. Rox pawed impatiently at the earth. Joe watched them admiringly.

"They've got spirit," he commented half to himself.

"I'm glad to have a horse to ride again," Mr. Jordan was saying. "The taxi driver wouldn't bring me any farther than the forked-roads crossing. Joe, here, came along and offered to bring me the rest of the way."

" 'Twas right on my way," Joe assured him. "I'm going up to Warner's."

Pinto laid his head on Montie's shoulder, and she reached up to stroke him. Tears were very near the surface as the horse rubbed his soft nose against her cheek, and she made an excuse to return to the house. No use to stand there and let them see her cry; maybe Joe had already noticed. He had looked at her rather curiously.

* * * * *

The days passed slowly after Pinto had been taken away. There was no pleasure in riding Rox or Nell. Although Montie could stay on all right, she had to be on the alert every second in order to do so. Besides, they were both exceedingly shy and at the least noise or movement in the underbrush along the mountain paths would wheel and gallop in the opposite direction.

And then one morning her father left for the day. It was not unusual for Montie to have charge of the place for hours at a time. Mr. Searles often had to ride quite long distances, buying and trading. Since her mother's death some years before, Montie had taken one responsibility after another as the need arose.

She had finished her lunch and attended to the wants of the horses and the little flock of poultry when a horse and rider appeared over the crest of the hill.

"Pinto!" she exclaimed aloud. "It can't be any other horse. I'd know that gait in a million!"

As the rider neared, she saw that it was not Mr. Jordan but Joe Elkins.

"Hello, Montie," saluted Joe. "Is your dad around?"

"No, he isn't," replied Montie, patting Pinto's smooth coat. "He went over Redthorn way this morning."

"To do a little dealing, I reckon," mused Joe. "And I've come to trade with him."

"I'm sorry he isn't here," said Montie. "But tell me, how does it happen that you are riding Pinto? Where is Mr. Jordan?"

"Well, it's like this," began Joe. "Jordan finds out that he isn't so good in the saddle. But he likes that little car I have, so we made a deal. Now he has the car, and I have his horse."

"But I thought you wanted a team."

"I do," answered Joe. "That's why I came over. I thought your dad might figure out a swap for those two blacks."

"Father said . . ."

"I know he held back the other day," agreed Joe, "but I hadn't a painted pony to offer then. You don't see so many of them these days, and they surely sell high. Besides, I figured you and your dad might be sort of attached to this one."

Rox and Nell stretched their heads over the fence curiously.

Montie looked from them to Pinto. If she traded even, it would be a good deal for her father. Montie hadn't lived on the horse-trading farm most of her life without learning values. And during the time they had boarded Pinto her father had had dozens of chances to sell him at a good price.

Montie had made a few trades of late, and her father had approved them. If she made this deal, she told herself that he would have to stay with it. He hadn't expressly told her not to let anyone have the blacks.

Still she hesitated.

"Huber has a team I could use. But he doesn't want Pinto very badly. Says his trade doesn't call for such high-class stuff."

Jud Huber, farther into the mountain country, handled a great many trades. It was said that Huber would make a deal somehow.

"Huber is coming to see me in the morning if he thinks he can figure out a swap," suggested Joe. "So if you want Pinto . . ."

"I *do* want Pinto!" cried Montie. "He's just the same as mine; I had him almost for my own for so long."

"Well, I don't think your dad ought to object if you deal with me."

Montie was wavering. Then suddenly she raised her head a little higher and spoke very decisively, "No, Joe, I can't trade. You don't know those blacks or you wouldn't want them. It would be a bad buy for you, and my father says a bad buy is seldom a good sale."

Joe looked disappointed. "Maybe you would buy Pinto outright then. I want you to have first chance."

"We can't afford it," replied Montie. "If you were going to keep him awhile—perhaps Father will have some cash deals soon."

Joe shook his head regretfully. "I can't do that. I need a team right away."

As Joe rode away, Pinto turned his head as if to inquire why Montie was letting him go.

Montie wished desperately to follow him—to shout at Joe—but at last she turned and walked slowly toward the house. Pinto was gone, and she had let him go. She had turned down her chance to keep him. In the morning Huber would visit Joe and undoubtedly lead Pinto away.

For the first time in her sturdy, honest life, Montie resented bitterly the ideals which she felt were keeping her father from making a lot of money. For the first time she hated the semi-tamed West, the glory of the thickly wooded mountains which rose in grand defiance on all sides. Why couldn't she have things she wanted? Why couldn't she have Pinto?

Because she was so engrossed in her thoughts she did not see another visitor until he jerked his horse to a stop in a little whirlwind of dust.

Wonderingly, Montie went to the gate.

Beneath the wide-brimmed hat smiled the bronzed face of Jim Merton, foreman of the Lazy Q Ranch near Redthorn Junction.

"I've come to get those two blacks," he informed her. "Here's the money. Count it while I introduce myself to them."

He tossed her a packet of bills with a slip of paper attached. On it was a note from her father.

"I sold him the blacks. The money is yours. Home before dark."

Montie's eyes shone as she counted the bills. A good price for the blacks. A good sale, and a good buy, for to the hard-riding cowboys on the Lazy Q, taming Rox and Nell would be only so much fun. They knew how to handle spirited horses. There were no restrictions when it came to dealing with the foreman of the Lazy Q. He knew horses, perhaps as well as Mr. Searles himself.

And then Jim Merton was back, leading the two blacks.

"By the way, your father asked me to tell you that he heard Joe Elkins has your painted pony."

"Oh, yes! Thank you. Joe was here today."

"Already, eh?"

"I wonder if you'd mind my riding Rox as far as Joe's place," said Montie.

"I'd be mighty glad for the company," replied Jim. "Save my leading her that far, too. Figuring to walk back, are you?"

There was a knowing twinkle in his eye as Montie's answer came very quickly: "No, not if I can make a deal with Joe!"

* * * * *

"Good Sale," by Caroline Young. Published April 19, 1936, in Young People's Weekly. *Reprinted by permission of Joe Wheeler (P.O. Box 1246, Conifer, Colorado 80422) and Cook Communication Ministries, Colorado Springs, Colorado. Caroline Young wrote for inspirational magazines during the first half of the twentieth century.*

The Seeing Eye

Will James

Dane Gruger was blind. Still, he knew every inch of his land and could ride the range on Little Eagle fully aware of everything that was happening around him.

Then came the big flood . . .

* * * * *

Will James was himself a western cowboy. This is written in his own vernacular.

* * * * *

It's worse than tough for anybody to be blind, but I don't think it's as tough for an indoor-born-and-raised person as it is for one whose life is all out of doors most of his life from childhood on. The outdoor man misses his freedom to roam over the hills and the sight of 'em ever changing. A canary would die outside his cage, but a free-born eagle would dwindle away inside of one.

Dane Gruger was very much of an out-of-door man. He was born on a little ranch along a creek bottom in the heart of the cow country; growed up with it to be a good cowboy, then, like with his dad, went on in the cow business. A railroad went through the lower part of the ranch, but stations and little towns was over twenty miles away either way.

He had a nice little spread when I went to work for him, was married and had two boys who done some of the riding. I'd been riding for Dane for quite a few days before I knew he was blind, not totally blind, but, as his boys told me, he couldn't see any further than his outstretched hand, and that was blurred. He couldn't read, not even big print, with any kind of glasses, so he never wore any.

That's what fooled me, and he could look you "right square in the eye" while talking to you. What was more, he'd go straight down to the corral, catch his horse, saddle him, and ride away like any man with full sight. The thing I first noticed and wondered at was that he never rode with us, and after the boys told me, I could understand. It was that he'd be of no use out on the range and away from the ranch.

Dane had been blind a few years when I come there, and he'd of course got to know every foot of the ten miles which the ranch covered on the creek bottom before that happened. The ranch itself was one to two miles wide in some places and taking in some brakes. The whole of that was fenced and cross-fenced into pastures and hay lands, and Dane knew to within an inch when he came to every fence, gate, or creek crossing. He knew how many head of cattle or horses might be in each pasture, how all was faring, when some broke out or some broke in, and where. He could find bogged cattle or a cow with a young calf needing help, and know everything that went well or wrong with what stock would be held on the ranch.

He, of course, seldom could do much towards helping whatever stock needed it or fix the holes he found in the fences, but when he'd get back to the ranch house he could easy tell the boys when there was anything wrong, and the exact spot where, in which field or pasture, how far from which side of the creek, or what fence, and what all the trouble might be. It would then be up to the boys to set things to rights, and after Dane's description of the spot, it was easy found.

During the time I was with that little outfit I got to know Dane pretty well, well enough to see that I don't think he could of lived if he hadn't been able to do what he was doing. He was so full of life and gumption and so appreciating of all around him that he could feel, hear, and breathe in. I'd sometimes see him hold his horse to a standstill while he only listened to birds or the faraway bellering of cattle, even to the yapping of prairie dogs which most cowboys would rather not hear the sound of.

To take him away from all of that, the open air, the feel of his saddle and horse under him, and set him on a chair to do nothing but sit and babble and think, would've brought a quick end to him.

With the riding he done, he felt satisfied he was doing something worth doing instead of just plain riding. He wouldn't of cared for that, and fact was, he well took the place of an average rider.

But he had mighty good help in the work he was doing, and that was the two horses he used, for they was both as well trained to his wants and care as the dogs that's used nowadays to lead the blind and which are called the seeing eye.

Dane had the advantage of the man with the dog, for he didn't have to walk and use a cane at every step. He rode, and he had more confidence in his horses' every step than he had in his own, even if he could of seen well. As horses do, they naturally sensed every foot of the earth under 'em without ever looking down at it, during sunlight, darkness, or under drifted snow.

Riding into clumps of willows or thickets, which the creek bottoms had much of, either of the two horses was careful to pick out a wide enough trail through so their rider wouldn't get scratched or brushed off. If they come to a place where the brush was too thick and Dane was wanting to go through that certain thicket, the ponies, regardless of his wants, would turn back for a ways and look for a better opening. Dane never argued with 'em at such times. He would just sort of head 'em where he wanted to go, and they'd do the rest to pick out the best way there.

Them horses was still young when I got to that outfit, seven and eight years of age, and would be fit for at least twenty years more with the little riding and good care they was getting. Dane's boys had broke 'em especially for their dad's use that way, and they'd done a fine job of it.

One of the horses, a gray of about a thousand pounds, was called Little Eagle. That little horse never missed a thing in sight or sound. With his training, the rustling of the brush close by would make him investigate and learn the cause before leaving that spot. Dane would know by his actions whether it was a new-born calf that had been hid or some cow in distress. It was the same at the boggy places along the creek or alkali swamps. If Little Eagle rode right on around and without stopping, Dane knew that all was well. If he stopped at any certain spot, bowed his neck and snorted low, then Dane knew that some horse or cow was in trouble. Keeping his hand on Little Eagle's neck he'd have him go on, and by the bend of that horse's neck as he went, like pointing, Dane could tell the exact location of where that animal was that was in trouble, or whatever it was that was wrong.

Sometimes, Little Eagle would line out on a trot, of his own accord and as though there was something needed looking into right away. At times he'd even break into a lope, and then Dane wouldn't know what to expect, whether it was stock breaking through a fence, milling around an animal that was down, or what. But most always it would be when a bunch of stock, horses or cattle, would be stringing out in single file, maybe going to water or some other part of the pasture.

At such times, Little Eagle would get just close enough to the stock so Dane could count 'em by the sounds of the hoofs going by, a near impossible thing to do for a man that can see, but Dane got so he could do it and get a mighty close count on what stock was in each pasture that way. Close enough so he could tell if any had got out or others got in.

With the horses in the pastures, there was bells on the leaders of every bunch and some on one of every little bunch that sort of held together and separate from others. Dane knew by the sound of every bell which bunch it was and about how many there would be to each. The boys kept him posted on that every time they'd run a bunch in for some reason or other. Not many horses was ever kept under fence, but there was quite a few of the purebred cattle for the upbreeding of the outside herds.

At this work of keeping tab on stock, Little Eagle was a cowboy by himself. With his natural intellect so developed as to what was wanted of him, he could near tell of what stock was wanted or not and where they belonged. The proof of that was when he turned a bunch of cattle out of a hayfield one time, and other times, and drove 'em to the gate of the field where they'd broke out of, circled around 'em when the gate was reached, and went to it for Dane to open. He then drove the cattle through; none got away, not from Little Eagle, and Dane would always prepare to ride at such times, for if any did try to break away, Little Eagle would be right on their tail to bring 'em back, and for a blind man, not knowing when his horse is going to break into a sudden run, stop, or turn, that's kind of hard riding, on a good cowhorse.

About all Dane would have to go by most of the time was the feel of the top muscles on Little Eagle's neck, and he got to know by them about the same as like language to him. With one hand most always on them muscles he felt what the horse seen. Tenseness, wonder, danger, fear, relaxation, and about all that a human feels at the sight of different things. Places, dangerous or smooth, trouble or peace.

Them top muscles told him more, and more plainly, than if another rider had been riding constantly alongside of him and telling him right along of what he seen. That was another reason why Dane liked to ride alone. He felt more at ease, no confusion, and wasn't putting anybody out of their way by talking and describing when they maybe wouldn't feel like it.

And them two horses of Dane's, they not only took him wherever he wanted to go, but never overlooked any work that needed to be done. They took it onto themselves to look for work which, being they always felt so good, was like play to them. Dane knew it when such times come, and he then would let 'em go as they chose.

Neither of the horses would, of course, go out by themselves without a rider and do that work. They wouldn't of been interested doing that without Dane's company. What's more they couldn't have opened the gates that had to be gone through, and besides they wasn't wanted to do that. They was to be the company of Dane and be with him in whatever he wanted to do.

Dane's other horse was a trim bay about the same size as Little Eagle, and even though just as good, he had different ways about him. He was called Ferret, and a ferret he was for digging up and finding out things, like a cow with new-born calf or mare with colt, and he was even better than Little Eagle for finding holes in fences or where some was down.

All that came under the special training the boys had given him and Little Eagle, and if it wasn't for automobiles these days, such as them would be mighty valuable companions in the city even more useful in the streets than the dog is, for the horse would soon know where his rider would want to go after being ridden such places a few times.

Unlike most horses it wasn't these two's nature to keep wanting to turn back to the ranch house when Dane would ride 'em away, and they wouldn't turn back until they knew the ride was over and it was time to. Sometimes Dane wouldn't show up for the noon meal, and that was all right with the ponies, too, for he'd often get off of 'em and let 'em graze with reins dragging. There was no danger of either of them ever leaving Dane, for they seemed as attached to him as any dog could be to his master.

It was the same way with Dane for them, and he had more confidence in their trueness and senses than most humans have in one another.

A mighty good test and surprising outcome of that came one day as a powerful big cloudburst hit above the ranch a ways and left Dane acrost the creek from home. The creek had turned into churning wild waters the size of a big river in a few minutes, half a mile wide in some places and licking up close to the higher land where the ranch buildings and corrals was.

It kept on a-raining hard after the cloudburst had fell, and it didn't act like it was going to let up for some time, and the wide river wouldn't be down to creek size or safe to cross, at least not for a day or so.

The noise of the rushing water was a-plenty to let Dane know of the cloudburst. It had come with a sudden roar and without a drop of warning, and Dane's horse, he was riding Little Eagle that day, plainly let him know the danger of the wide stretch of swirling fast waters. It wasn't the danger of the water only but uprooted trees and all kinds of heavy timber speeding along would make the crossing more than dangerous, not only dangerous but it would about mean certain death.

Little Eagle would of tackled the swollen waters or anything Dane would of wanted him to, but Dane knew a whole lot better than to make that wise horse go where he didn't want to, any time.

Dane could tell by the noise, and riding to the edge of the water and the location where he was, how wide the body of wild waters was. He knew that the stock could keep out of reach of it on either side without being jammed against the fences, but he got worried about the ranch, wondering if the waters had got up to the buildings. He worried, too, about his family worrying about him and maybe trying to find and get to him.

That worrying got him to figuring on ways of getting back. He sure couldn't stay where he was until the waters went down, not if he could help it. It wouldn't be comfortable being out so long in the heavy rain either, even if he did have his slicker on, and it wouldn't do to try to go to the neighbor's ranch which was some fifteen miles away. He doubted if he could find it anyway, for it was acrost a bunch of rolling hills, with nothing to go by, and Little Eagle wouldn't know that *there* would be where Dane would be wanting him to go. Besides there was the thought of his family worrying so about him and maybe risking their lives in trying to find him.

He'd just have to get home, somehow, and it was at the thought of his neighbor's ranch and picturing the distance and country to it in his mind, that he thought of the railroad, for he would of had to cross it to get there, and then, thinking of the railroad, the thought came of the trestle crossing along it and over the creek. Maybe he could make that. That would be sort of a dangerous crossing, too, but the more he thought of it, the more he figured it worth taking the chances of trying. That was the only way of his getting on the other side of the high waters and back to the ranch.

The railroad and trestle was only about half a mile from where he now was, and that made it all the more tempting to try. So, after thinking it over in every way, including the fact that he'd be taking chances with losing his horse also, he finally decided to take the chance, at the risk of both himself and his horse, that is, if his horse seen it might be safe enough. He felt it had to be done and it could be done. He had faith and confidence in that Little Eagle horse of his.

And that confidence sure wasn't misplaced, for, a cooler-headed, brainier horse never was.

There was two fences to cross to get to the railroad and trestle, and it wasn't at all necessary to go through gates to get there, for the swollen waters with jamming timbers had laid the fence down for quite a ways on both sides of the wide river and caused some of the wire strands to break and snap and coil all directions.

A strand of barbed wire, even if flat to the ground, is a mighty dangerous thing to ride over, for a horse might pick it up with a hoof, and, as most horses will scare, draw their hind legs up under 'em and act up. The result might be a wicked sawing wire cut at the joint by the hock, cutting veins and tendons and often crippling a horse for life. In such cases the rider is also very apt to get tangled up in the wire, for that wicked stuff seems to have the ways of the tentacles of a devilfish at such times.

Loose wire laying around on the ground is the cowboys' worst fear, especially so with Dane, for, as he couldn't see, it was many times more threatening as he rode most every day from one fenced-in field to the other. But the confidence he had in his two cool-headed ponies relieved him of most all his fear of the dangerous barbed wire, and either one of 'em would stop and snort a little at the sight of a broken strand coiled on the ground. Dane knew what that meant, and it always brought a chill to his spine. He'd get down off his saddle, feel around carefully in front of his horse, and usually the threatening coil would be found to within a foot or so of his horse's nose. The coil would then be pulled and fastened to the fence, to stay until a ranch hand who, with team and buckboard, would make the rounds of all fences every few months, done a general fixing of 'em.

It's too bad barbed wire *has* to be used for fences. It has butchered and killed many good horses and some riders. But barbed wire is about the only kind of fence that will hold cattle, most of the time, and when there has to be many long miles of it, even with the smaller ranches, that's about the only kind of fence that can be afforded or used. Cattle (even the wildest) seldom get a scratch by it, even in breaking through a four-strand fence of it, or going over it while it's loose and coiled on the ground, for they don't get rattled when in wire as a horse does, and they hold their hind legs straight back when going through, while with the horse he draws 'em under him instead and goes to tearing around.

Both Little Eagle and Ferret had been well trained against scaring and fighting wire if they ever got into it, also trained not to get into it, and stop whenever coming to some that was loose on the ground. That training had been done with a rope and a piece of smooth wire at one end, and being they was naturally cool-headed they soon learned all the tricks of the wire and how to behave when they come near any of that coiled on the ground.

There was many such coils as the flood waters rampaged along the creek bottom, and as Dane headed Little Eagle towards the railroad and trestle he then let him pick his own way through and around the two fence entanglements on the way there, along the edge of the rushing water.

Little Eagle done considerable winding around and careful stepping as he come to the fences that had been snapped and washed to scattering, dangerous strands over the field. Dane gave him his time, let him go as he choose, and finally the roar of the waters against the high banks by the trestle came to his ears. It sounded as though it was near up to the trestle, which he knew was plenty high, and that gave him a good idea of what a cloudburst it had been.

He then got mighty dubious about trying to cross the trestle, for it was a long one, there was no railing of any kind on the sides, and part of it might be under water or even washed away. There was some of the flood water in the ditch alongside the railroad grade, and it wasn't so many feet up it to the track level.

Riding between the rails a short ways he come to where the trestle began, and there he stopped Little Eagle. The swirling waters made a mighty roar right there, and how he wished he could of been able to see then, more than any time since his blindness had overtook him.

Getting off Little Eagle there, he felt his way along to the first ties to the trestle, of the space between each, which was about five inches, and just right for Little Eagle's small hoofs to slip in between, Dane thought. One such a slip would mean a broken leg, and the horse would have to be shot right there, to lay between the rails. The rider would be mighty likely to go over the side of the trestle, too.

Dane hardly had any fear for himself, but he did have for Little Eagle. Not that he feared he would put a foot between the ties, for that little horse was too wise, cool-headed, and careful to do anything like that, Dane knew. What worried him most was whether the trestle was still up and above water all the way acrost. There would be no turning back, for in turning is when Little Eagle would be mighty liable to slip a hoof between the ties. The rain had let up, but the wind was blowing hard, and the tarred ties was slippery as soaped glass.

It all struck Dane as fool recklessness to try to cross on that long and narrow trestle at such a time, but he felt he should try, and to settle his dubiousness he now left it to Little Eagle and his good sense as to whether to tackle it or not.

If he went, he would *ride* him across, not try to crawl, feel his way, and lead him, for in being led Little Eagle wouldn't be apt to pay as much attention to his footing and to nosing every dangerous step he made. Besides, Dane kind of felt that if Little Eagle should go over the side he'd go with him.

So, getting into the saddle again, he let Little Eagle stand for a spell, at the same time letting him know that he wanted to cross the trestle, for him to size it up and see if it could be done. It was up to him, and the little gray well understood.

It might sound unbelievable, but a good sensible horse and rider have a sort of feel-language which is mighty plain between 'em, and when comes a particular dangerous spot the two can discuss the possibilities of getting over or acrost it as well as two humans can, and even better, for the horse has the instinct which the human lacks. He can tell danger where the human can't, and the same with the safety.

It was that way with Little Eagle and Dane, only even more so, because as Little Eagle, like Ferret, had been trained to realize Dane's affliction, cater to and sort of take care of him, they was always watchful. Then with Dane's affection and care for them, talking to 'em and treating 'em like the true pardners they was, there was an understanding and trust between man and horse that's seldom seen between man and man.

Dane sat in the saddle with his hand on Little Eagle's neck, and the two "discussed" the dangerous situation ahead in such a way that the loud roar of the water foaming by and under the trestle didn't interfere any with the decision that was to come.

There was a tenseness in the top muscles of Little Eagle's neck as he looked over the scary, narrow, steel-ribboned trail ahead, nervous at the so careful investigation, that all sure didn't look well. But Dane had now left it all to Little Eagle's judgment, and just as he had about expected Little Eagle would be against trying, the horse, still all tense and quivering some, planted one foot on the first tie, and crouching a bit, all nerves and muscles steady, started on the way of the dangerous crossing.

Every step by step from the first seemed like a long minute to Dane. The brave little horse, his nose close to the ties, at the same time looking ahead, was mighty careful how he placed each front foot, and sure that the hind one would come up to the exact same place afterwards, right where that front one had been. He didn't just plank his hoof and go on, but felt for a sure footing on the wet and slippery tarred ties before putting any weight on it and making another step. Something like a mountain climber feeling and making sure of his every hold while going on with his climbing.

The start wasn't the worst of the crossing. That begin to come as they went further along and nearer to the center. There, with the strong wind blowing broadside of 'em, the swift waters churning, sounding like to the level of the slippery ties, would seem about scary enough to chill the marrow in any being. But there was more piled onto that, for as they neared the center it begin to tremble and sway as if by earth tremors. This was by the high rushing waters swirling around the tall and now submerged supporting timbers.

Little Eagle's step wasn't so sure then, and as careful as he was there come a few times when he slipped, and a time or two when a hoof went down between the ties, leaving him to stand on three shaking legs until he got his hoof up and on footing again.

With most any other horse it would of been the end of him and his rider right then. As it was, Little Eagle went on, like a tightrope walker, with every muscle at work. And Dane, riding mighty light on him, his heart up his throat at every slip or loss of footing, done his best not to get him off balance but help him that way when he thought he could.

If the shaking, trembling, and swaying of the trestle had been steady it would of been less scary and some easier, but along with the strong vibrations of the trestle there'd sometimes come a big uprooted tree to smash into it at a forty-mile speed. There'd be a quiver all along the trestle at the impact. It would sway and bend dangerously, to slip back again as the tree would be washed under and on.

Such goings on would jar Little Eagle's footing to where he'd again slip a hoof between the ties, and Dane would pray, sometimes cuss a little. But the way Little Eagle handled his feet and every part of himself, sometimes on the tip of his toes, the sides of his hoofs and even to his knees, he somehow managed to keep right side up.

Good thing, Dane thought, *that the horse wasn't shod, for shoes without sharp calks would have been much worse on than none on the slippery ties.* As it was, and being his shoes had been pulled off only a couple of days before to ease his feet some between shoeings, his hoofs was sharp at the edges and toe, and that gave him more chance.

The scary and most dangerous part of the trestle was reached, the center, and it was a good thing maybe that Dane couldn't see while Little Eagle sort of juggled himself over that part, for the trestle had been under repair and some of the old ties had been taken away in a few places, to later be replaced by new ones; but where each tie had been taken away that left an opening of near two feet wide. Mighty scary for Little Eagle too, but he eased over them gaps without Dane knowing.

Dane felt as though it was long weary miles and took about that much time to finally get past the center and most dangerous part of the five-hundred-yard trestle, for them five hundred yards put more wear on him during that time than five hundred miles would of.

And he was far from near safe going as yet, for he'd just passed center, and the trestle was still doing some tall trembling and dangerous weaving, when, as bad and spooky as things already was, there come the sound of still worse fear and danger, and Dane's heart stood still. It was a train whistle he'd heard above the roar of the waters. It sounded like the train was coming his way, facing him, and there'd sure be no chance for him to turn and make it back, for he'd crossed over half of the trestle, the worst part, and going back would take a long time.

All the dangers and fears piling together now, instead of exciting Dane, seemed to cool and steady him, like having to face the worst and make the best of it. He rode right on towards the coming train.

He knew from memory that the railroad run a straight line to the trestle, that there was no railroad crossing nor other reason for the engineer to blow his whistle, unless it was for him, himself. Then it came to him that the engineer must of seen him on the trestle and would sure stop his train if he could.

Standing up in his stirrups he raised his big black hat high as he could and waved it from side to side as a signal for the engineer to stop his train. Surely they could see that black hat of his and realize the predicament he was in. That getting off the trestle would mean almost certain death.

But the train sounded like it was coming right on, and at that Dane wondered if maybe it was coming too fast to be able to stop. He got a little panicky then, and for a second he was about to turn Little Eagle off the trestle and swim for it. It would of been a long and risky swim, maybe carried for miles down country before they could of reached either bank, and it would of taken more than luck, to have succeeded. But if they'd got bowled over by some tree trunk and went down the churning waters, that would be better, Dane thought, than to have Little Eagle smashed to smithereens by the locomotive. He had no thought for himself.

About the only thing that made him take a bigger chance and ride on some more was that he knew that the whole train and its crew would be doomed before it got halfways on the trestle, and what if it was a passenger train?

At that thought he had no more fear of Little Eagle keeping his footing on the trestle. His fear now went for the many lives there might be on the train, and he sort of went wild and to waving his big black hat all the more in trying to warn of the danger.

But he didn't put on no such action as to unbalance the little gray in any way. He still felt and helped with his every careful step, and then there got to be a prayer with each one, like with the beads of the rosary.

He rubbed his moist eyes and also prayed he could see, now of all times and if only just for this once, and then the train whistle blew again, so close this time that it sounded like it was on the trestle, like coming on, and being mighty near to him. Dane had done his best, and now was his last and only chance to save Little Eagle and himself, by sliding off the trestle. He wiped his eyes like as though to better see, and went to reining Little Eagle off the side of the trestle. But to his surprise, Little Eagle wouldn't respond to the rein. It was the first time excepting amongst the thick brush or bad creek crossings that horse had ever went against his wishes that way. But this was now very different, and puzzled, he tried him again and again, with no effect, and then, all at once, *he could see.*

* * * * *

Myself and one of Dane's boys had been riding, looking for Dane soon after the cloudburst hit, and seeing the stopped passenger train with the many people gathered by the engine we high-loped towards it, there to get the surprise of seeing Dane on Little Eagle on the trestle and carefully making each and every dangerous step towards us and solid ground.

We seen we sure couldn't be of no use to the little gray nor Dane, only maybe a hindrance, and being there was only a little ways more we held our horses and watched. Looking on the length of the trestle we noticed that only the rails and ties showed above the high water, there was quite a bend in it from the swift and powerful pressure, and the rails and ties was leaning, like threatening to break loose at any time.

How the little horse and Dane ever made it, with the strong wind, slippery ties, and all a-weaving, was beyond us. So was it with the passengers who stood with gaping mouths and tense watching. What if they'd known that the rider had been blind while he made the dangerous crossing?

And as the engineer went on to tell the spellbound passengers how that man and horse on the trestle had saved all their lives, they was more than thankful, for, as the heavy cloudburst had come so sudden and hit in one spot, there'd been no report of it, and, as the engineer said, he might of drove onto the trestle a ways before knowing. Then it would of been too late.

But Little Eagle was the one who played the biggest part in stopping what would have been a terrible happening. He was the one who decided to make the dangerous crossing, the one who had to use his head and hoofs with all his skill and power, also the one who at the last of the stretch would not heed Dane's pull of the reins to slide off the trestle. His first time not to do as Dane wanted him to. He'd disobeyed and had saved another life. He'd been the seeing eye.

The fuss over with as Dane finally rode up on solid ground and near the engine, we then was the ones due for a big surprise. For Dane *spotted* us out from the crowd, and smiling, rode straight for us and looked us both "square in the eye."

The shock and years he lived crossing that trestle, then the puzzling over Little Eagle not wanting to turn at the touch of the rein had done the trick, had brought his sight back.

After that day, Little Eagle and Ferret was sort of neglected, neglected knee deep in clover, amongst good shade and where clear spring water run. The seeing eyes was partly closed in contentment.

* * * * *

"The Seeing Eye," by Will James. Published in many anthologies, including James's 1940 collection, Horses I Have Known. *If anyone knows of earliest appearance of this old story, please contact Joe Wheeler (P.O. Box 1246, Conifer, Colorado 80433). Will James (1892–1942) was born in Great Falls, Montana, was a western cowboy himself for many years, and later wrote a number of books depicting the cowboy life. His best known include* Smoky, the Cowhorse; Lone Cowboy; *and* Uncle Bill.

THE WHITE HORSE OF SAXONY

Mary Kathryn Kent

In a raging storm, a man of gigantic stature was forced to ask for shelter at a rude mountain hut. Reluctantly, the host offered hospitality to his unexpected guest.

But later, he had second thoughts.

* * * * *

Every boy and girl who knows anything of history has heard of the great Charlemagne, whose empire extended over nearly all western Europe. In Italy, Spain, and southern Germany, he was alike victorious over his enemies.

The Saxons, however, refused to submit to his rule. They were a brave, barbarous people who believed in the old heathen gods and hated most bitterly the Christianity which Charlemagne proposed.

Long and desperate was the war. For thirty-two years it raged, with few intermissions. Sometimes Charlemagne would be victorious, and the Saxons would seem conquered; but no sooner was Charlemagne engaged in war elsewhere, than they would gather under their native chiefs and renew the struggle. The greatest cruelty was shown to the Saxons; they were carried away into foreign lands; their country was laid waste; and at one time, as a punishment for rebellion, forty-five hundred who had been taken prisoners were put to death.

All this barbarity, however, only made the Saxons more determined in their resistance. Their leader, the brave Wittekind, was once obliged to seek protection in Denmark, but he soon returned to lead his people against their conqueror. Two bloody battles were fought, in the last of which the Saxons were defeated. Soon after this, they submitted. Wittekind and his wife, Gera, were baptized, Charlemagne being sponsor.

From this time on Saxony became tranquil under the rule of Charlemagne, and Christianity was accepted as its religion. Historians tell us that the leaders became convinced that heaven was on the side of Charlemagne, and so yielded. German tradition explains more fully this sudden change on the part of the Saxons.

* * * * *

A thunderstorm at evening, so runs the legend, had followed a warm summer day. The thunder rolled; the wind swept through the tops of the ancient oaks. The waters of the Weser foamed and dashed against a little hut that stood upon its banks, as if they would wash it away. In the door of the hut a Saxon of powerful frame stood looking out at the raging storm. Suddenly he saw, making its way through the underbrush, the figure of a man. The newcomer was of gigantic stature, but his torn clothing and bewildered glance showed him to be one who had lost his way. Soon as he spied the hut, his countenance lighted with a smile.

"Can I find here a shelter? Will you lodge me?" he cried, coming toward the hut.

The man in the door looked distrustful as he asked, "You are lost in the woods? You are a stranger in this region?"

"Since morning I have wandered among the mountains, not knowing how to find my way out. Now I desire a lodging where I can await the morning, which, God willing, shall bring me again to my own people."

The expression of distrust did not leave the face of the Saxon, and the duty which hospitality laid upon him was evidently a distasteful one.

"Be welcome," he said, slowly advancing toward the stranger; "come under the shelter of my hut."

The guest seemed to find but little more pleasure in accepting the invitation than the Saxon had in extending it. He glanced with evident disquiet around the apartment, whose walls were adorned with images of the heathen divinities and the stone weapons of the Saxons. Soon, however, his countenance cleared, and after partaking of a repast which his host placed before him, he threw himself on the bearskin bed and was soon asleep.

Long after his guest slept, the Saxon sat brooding by the fire. Suddenly seizing his stone knife, he started from his seat but, with a glance at the image of his god, dropped back again.

"No, no! Woden commands that the rights of hospitality be honored. It must not be."

So speaking, he cast himself upon his bearskin and was soon asleep.

All signs of the tempest had vanished when the bright rays of the morning sun awakened the two sleepers. Hastily springing up, they put in order their dress and ate together their simple breakfast.

"God reward you for the shelter and food you have given me!" said the guest. "Permit me now to take my departure."

"I will accompany you," said the Saxon. "I know every outlet of this country."

As they journeyed, the stranger saw gamboling on the green meadow a beautiful white horse. "See," he cried, "this fine horse. Let us catch and tame him."

"He will not easily be caught or tamed," replied the Saxon.

"Why not?" said the stranger. "Give me a cord; he shall soon know me as master."

"You can try it," was the answer, "but you will soon find that your trouble is vain. This wild horse will never yield to power, but if you show kindness, he will come of his own free will." So saying, he motioned with his hand.

The beautiful beast raised his head, then began slowly to approach them. The Saxon patted his slender neck, and stroking lovingly his silver white mane, he said, "In this horse you see a symbol of the free, unconquered Saxon people; they will never yield to power. Before we allow ourselves to be compelled to honor the Christ-God whom you Franks are striving to bring into our land with fire and sword, we will die to the last man."

"But if I try love, if I use gentleness?" said the stranger, half to himself, as he watched the horse rubbing his head against the Saxon's shoulder.

"The Franks know only how to use rough power," replied the Saxon gloomily.

"But it shall be otherwise," cried the other; "the war shall end, and peace shall unite both peoples. My word that it shall be done," he continued, raising his hand with regal mien to the heavens, "my imperial word as a pledge, for know I am Charles, Emperor of Germany!"

"Do you think that I have not known you? This majestic form, these golden locks, these sparkling blue eyes, would betray you among a thousand. When last night you stood before my threshold, I knew that it was the deadly enemy of my people who begged shelter."

"You knew me," said the emperor, "and still received me with hospitality?"

"Although I would gladly have buried my knife in your breast, I harmed no hair of your head, for Woden commands, 'Your guest shall be holy to you.' "

"I, too, soon knew that I was under the roof of an enemy," said the emperor; "but I believed myself unknown and trusted to my strength for protection. But who art thou? Thy clothing, thy imperious look, thy noble bearing, show thee no common man."

"I am Wittekind," replied the Saxon. "Wittekind, the leader of my people."

"Blessed be the hour which brought us together, and blessed be the white horse that has given me this example of the power of mildness!" cried the emperor, seizing the hand of the Saxon prince. "In peace shall Frank and Saxon dwell together, and no more through the power of the sword, but through persuasion, through love, will I seek to spread Christianity among you."

"And I," replied Wittekind, conquered by the friendly words of the emperor, "I promise allegiance for myself and my people. We will hear the message of the Christ-God whom you could never have forced us to obey."

The pledges of Charlemagne and Wittekind were fulfilled. There was peace between the two peoples, and gradually the Saxons accepted the religion of gentleness and love and became Christians. Wittekind remained a true vassal of the emperor and bore on his shield an image of the white horse that had wrought this change to his people.

Centuries have passed. The Saxons bear another name and have in customs and manners become another people. But today the white horse of the old tradition, the emblem of early Saxon freedom, is the device on the crest of Brunswick and Hanover.

* * * * *

"The White Horse of Saxony," by Mary Kathryn Kent. Published October 19, 1926, in The Youth's Instructor. *Reprinted by permission of Joe Wheeler (P.O. Box 1246, Conifer, Colorado 80433) and Review and Herald® Publishing Association, Hagerstown, Maryland. Mary Kathryn Kent wrote for popular and inspirational magazines during the first half of the twentieth century.*

Illustration on page 150 used by permission of the artist, Ashley Applegate.

Coaly-Bay, the Outlaw Horse

Ernest Thompson Seton

Over time, the true story of Coaly-Bay has gradually become an American classic, one of the most popular horse stories ever written.

* * * * *

The willful beauty

Five years ago in the Bitterroot mountains of Idaho there was a beautiful little foal. His coat was bright bay; his legs, mane, and tail were glossy black—coal black and bright bay—so they called him Coaly-bay.

"Coaly-bay" sounds like "Koli-bey," which is an Arab title of nobility, and those who saw the handsome colt and did not know how he came by the name, thought he must be of Arab blood. No doubt he was, in a far-away sense, just as all our best horses have Arab blood, and once in a while it seems to have come out strong and show in every part of the creature, in his frame, his power, and his wild, free, roving spirit.

Coaly-bay loved to race like the wind; he gloried in his speed, his tireless legs, and when careering with the herd of colts they met a fence or ditch, it was as natural to Coaly-bay to overleap it as it was for the others to sheer off.

So he grew up strong of limb, restless of spirit, and rebellious at any thought of restraint. Even the kindly curb of the hay yard or the stable was unwelcome, and he soon showed that he would rather stand out all night in a driving storm than be locked in a comfortable stall where he had no vestige of the liberty he loved so well.

He became very clever at dodging the horse wrangler whose job it was to bring the horse herd to the corral. The very sight of that man set Coaly-bay a going. He became what is known as a "quit the bunch"—that is a horse of such independent mind that he will go his own way the moment he does not like the way of the herd.

So each month the colt became more set on living free and more cunning in the means he took to win his way. Far down in his soul, too, there must have been a streak of cruelty, for he stuck at nothing and spared no one that seemed to stand between him and his one desire.

When he was three years of age, just in the perfection of his young strength and beauty, his real troubles began, for now his owner undertook to break him to ride. He was as tricky and vicious as he was handsome, and the first day's experience was a terrible battle between the horse trainer and the beautiful colt.

But the man was skillful. He knew how to apply his power, and all the wild plunging, bucking, rearing, and rolling of the wild one had no desirable result. With all his strength the horse was hopelessly helpless in the hands of the skillful horseman, and Coaly-bay was so far mastered at length that a good rider could use him. But each time the saddle went on, he made a new fight. After a few months of this, the colt seemed to realize that it was useless to resist, that it simply won for him lashings and spurrings, so he pretended to reform. For a week he was ridden each day, and not once did he buck, but on the last day he came home lame.

His owner turned him out to pasture. Three days later he seemed all right; he was caught and saddled. He did not buck, but within five minutes he went lame as before. Again he was turned out to pasture, and after a week, saddled, only to go lame again.

His owner did not know what to think, whether the horse really had a lame leg or was only shamming, but he took the first chance to get rid of him, and though Coaly-bay was easily worth fifty dollars, he sold him for twenty-five. The new owner felt he had a bargain, but after being ridden half a mile Coaly-bay went lame. The rider got off to examine the foot, whereupon Coaly-bay broke away and galloped back to his old pasture. Here he was caught, and the new owner, being neither gentle nor sweet,

applied spur without mercy, so that the next twenty miles were covered in less than two hours and no sign of lameness appeared.

Now they were at the ranch of this new owner. Coaly-bay was led from the door of the house to the pasture, limping all the way, and then turned out. He limped over to the other horses. On one side of the pasture was the garden of a neighbor. The man was very proud of his fine vegetables and had put a six-foot fence around the place. Yet the very night after Coaly-bay arrived, certain of the horses got into the garden somehow and did a great deal of damage. But they leaped out before daylight, and no one saw them.

The gardener was furious, but the ranch man stoutly maintained that it must have been some other horses, since his were behind a six-foot fence.

The next night it happened again. The ranch man went out very early and saw all his horses in the pasture, with Coaly-bay behind them. His lameness seemed worse now instead of better. In a few days, however, the horse was seen walking all right, so the ranch man's son caught him and tried to ride him. But this seemed too good a chance to lose; all his old wickedness returned to the horse; the boy was bucked off at once and hurt. The ranch man himself now leaped into the saddle; Coaly-bay bucked for ten minutes, but finding he could not throw the man, he tried to crush his leg against a post, but the rider guarded himself well. Coaly-bay reared and threw himself backward; the rider slipped off, the horse fell, jarring heavily, and before he could rise the man was in the saddle again. The horse now ran away, plunging and bucking; he stopped short, but the rider did not go over his head, so Coaly-bay turned, seized the man's foot in his teeth and but for heavy blows on the nose would have torn him dreadfully. It was quite clear now that Coaly-bay was an "outlaw"—that is, an incurably vicious horse.

The saddle was jerked off, and he was driven, limping, into the pasture.

The raids on the garden continued, and the two men began to quarrel over it. But to prove that his horses were not guilty the ranch man asked the gardener to sit up with him and watch. That night as the moon was brightly shining they saw, not all the horses, but Coaly-bay, walk straight up to the garden fence—no sign of a limp now—easily leap over it, and proceed to gobble the finest things he could find. After they had made sure of his identity, the men ran forward. Coaly-bay cleared the fence like a deer, lightly raced over the pasture to mix with the horse herd, and when the men came near him he had—oh, such an awful limp.

"That settles it," said the rancher. "He's a fraud, but he's a beauty and good stuff, too."

"Yes, but it settles who took my garden truck," said the other.

"Well, I suppose so," was the answer; "but look here, neighbor, you haven't more than ten dollars in truck. The horse is easily worth—a hundred. Give me twenty-five dollars, take the horse, and call it square."

"Not much I will," said the gardener. "I'm out twenty-five dollars worth of truck; the horse isn't worth a cent more. I take him and call it even."

And so the thing was settled. The ranch man said nothing about Coaly-bay being vicious as well as cunning, but the gardener found out the very first time he tried to ride him that the horse was as bad as he was beautiful.

The next day a sign appeared on the gardener's gate:

FOR SALE
First class horse
Sound and gentle—$10.00

The bear bait

Now at this time a band of hunters came riding by. There were three mountaineers, two men from the city, and the writer of this story. The city men were going to hunt bear. They had guns and everything needed for bear hunting, except bait. It is usual to buy some worthless horse or cow, drive it into the mountains where the bears are, and kill it there. So seeing the sign up, the hunters called to the gardener: "Haven't you got a cheaper horse?"

The gardener replied: "Look at him there, isn't he a beauty? You won't find a cheaper horse if you travel a thousand miles."

"We are looking for an old bear bait, and five dollars is our limit," replied the hunters.

Horses were cheap and plentiful in that country; buyers were scarce. The gardener feared that Coaly-bay would escape. "Well, if that's the best you can do, he's yours."

The hunters handed him five dollars, then said, "Now, stranger, bargain's settled. Will you tell us why you sell this fine horse for five dollars?"

"Mighty simple. He can't be ridden. He's dead lame when he's going your way and sound as a dollar going his own; no fence in the country can hold him; he's a dangerous outlaw. He's wickeder than old Nick."

"Well, he's an almighty handsome bear bait," said the hunters and rode on.

Coaly-bay was driven with the packhorses and limped dreadfully on the trail. Once or twice he tried to go back, but he was easily turned by the men behind him. His limp grew worse, and toward night it was painful to see him.

The leading guide remarked, "That limp ain't no fake. He's got some deep-seated trouble."

Day after day the hunters rode farther into the mountains, driving the horses along and hobbling them at night. Coaly-bay went with the rest, limping along, tossing his head and his long splendid mane at every step. One of the hunters tried to ride him and nearly lost his life, for the horse seemed possessed of a demon as soon as the man was on his back.

The road grew harder as it rose. A very bad bog had to be crossed one day. Several horses were mired in it, and as the men rushed to the rescue, Coaly-bay saw his chance of escape. He wheeled in a moment and turned himself from a limping, low-headed, sorry, bad-eyed creature into a high-spirited horse. Head and tail aloft now, shaking their black streamers in the wind, he gave a joyous neigh, and without a trace of lameness, dashed for his home one hundred miles away, threading each narrow trail with perfect certainty, though he had seen them but once before, and in a few minutes he had steamed away from their sight.

The men were furious, but one of them, saying not a word, leaped on his horse—to do what? Follow that free-ranging racer? Sheer folly. Oh, no! He knew a better plan. He knew the country. Two miles around by the trail, half a mile by the rough cutoff that he took, was Panther Gap. The runaway must pass through that, and Coaly-bay raced down the trail to find the guide below awaiting him. Tossing his head with anger, he wheeled on up the trail again and within a few yards recovered his monotonous limp and his evil expression. He was driven into camp, and there he vented his rage by kicking in the ribs of a harmless little packhorse.

His destined end

This was bear country, and the hunters resolved to end his dangerous pranks and make him useful for once. They dared not catch him; it was not really safe to go near him. But two of the guides drove him to a distant glade where bears abounded. A thrill of pity came over me as I saw that beautiful untamable creature going away with his imitation limp.

"Aren't you coming along?" called the guide.

"No, I don't want to see him die," was the answer. Then as the tossing head was disappearing I called, "Say, fellows, I wish you would bring me back that mane and tail when you come back!"

Fifteen minutes later a distant rifle crack was heard, and in my mind's eye I saw that proud head and those superb limbs, robbed of their sustaining indomitable spirit, falling flat and limp—to suffer the unsightly end of fleshly things. Poor Coaly-bay; he would not bear the yoke. Rebellious to the end, he had fought against the fate of all his kind. It seemed to me the spirit of an eagle or a wolf it was that dwelt behind those full bright eyes, that ordered all his wayward life.

I tried to put the tragic finish out of mind and had not long to battle with the thought—not even one short hour—for the men came back.

Down the long trail to the west they had driven him; there was no chance for him to turn aside. He must go on, and the men behind felt safe in that.

Farther away from his old home on the Bitterroot River he had gone each time he journeyed. And now he had passed the high divide and was keeping the narrow trail that leads to the valley of bears and on to Salmon River and still away to the open wild Columbian Plains, limping sadly as though he knew. His glossy hide flashed back the golden sunlight, still richer than it fell, and the men behind followed like hangmen in the death train of a nobleman condemned—down the narrow trail till it opened into a little beaver meadow with rank rich grass, a lovely mountain stream, and winding bear paths up and down the waterside.

"Guess this'll do," said the older man. "Well, here goes for a sure death or a clean miss," said the other confidently, and waiting till the limper was out in the middle of the meadow, he gave a short, sharp whistle. Instantly Coaly-bay was alert. He swung and faced his tormentors, his noble head erect, his nostrils flaring—a picture of horse beauty, yes, of horse perfection.

The rifle was leveled, the very brain its mark, just on the cross line of the eyes and ears, that meant sure, sudden, painless death.

The rifle cracked. The great horse wheeled and dashed away. It was sudden death or miss—and the marksman *missed.*

Away went the wild horse at his famous best, not for his eastern home, but down the unknown western trail, away and away; the pine woods hid him from view, and left behind was the rifleman vainly trying to force the empty cartridge from his gun.

Down that trail with an inborn certainty he went and on through the pines, then leaped a great bog, and splashed an hour later through the limpid Clearwater and on, responsive to some unknown guide that subtly called him from the farther west. And so he went till the dwindling pines gave place to scrubby cedars and these in turn were mixed with sage, and onward still, till the faraway flat plains of Salmon River were about him, and ever on, tireless as it seemed, he went, and crossed the canyon of the mighty Snake, and up again to the high wild plains where the wire fence still is not, and on, beyond the Buffalo Hump, till moving specks on the far horizon caught his eager eyes, and coming on and near, they moved and rushed aside to wheel and face about. He lifted up his voice and called to them, the long shrill neigh of his kindred when they bugled to each other on the far Chaldean plain. And back their answer came. This way and that they wheeled and sped and caracoled, and Coaly-bay drew nearer, called and gave the countersigns his kindred know, till this they were assured—he was their kind, he was of the wild free blood that man had never tamed. And when night came down on the purpling plain his place was in the herd as one who after many a long hard journey in the dark had found his home.

There you may see him yet, for still his strength endures, and his beauty is not less. The riders tell me they have seen him many times in Cedra. He is swift and strong among the swift ones, but it is that flowing mane and tail that mark him chiefly from afar.

There on the wild free plains of sage he lives; the storm wind smites his glossy coat at night, and the winter snows are driven hard on him at times; the wolves are there to harry all the weak ones of the herd, and in the spring the mighty grizzly, too, may come to claim his toll. There are no luscious pastures made by man, no grain foods; nothing but the wild hard hay, the wind and the open plains, but here at last he found the thing he craved—the one worth all the rest. Long may he roam—this is my wish. And this—that I may see him once again in all the glory of his speed with his black mane on the wind, the spur-galls gone from his flanks, and in his eye the blazing light that grew in his far-off forebears' eyes as they spurned Arabian plains to leave behind the racing wild beast and the fleet gazelle—yes, too, the driving sandstorm that overwhelmed the rest, but strove in vain on the dusty wake of the desert's highest born.

* * * * *

"Coaly-Bay, the Outlaw Horse," by Ernest Thompson Seton. Published in Seton's Wild Animal Ways *(Doubleday, 1916). Text owned by Joe Wheeler. Ernest Thompson Seton (1860–1946) was born in South Shields, England, and moved to Canada in 1866. Seton is considered to be the founder of animal fiction writing as well as a prolific writer of true nature stories. He was instrumental in founding the Boy Scouts of America and the organization Woodcraft Indians. Among his books are bestsellers such as* Wild Animals I Have Known *and* Animal Heroes.

If you enjoyed this book, you'll enjoy these others in The Good Lord Made Them All series from editor/compiler Joe L. Wheeler.

Owney, the Post Office Dog
and Other Great Dog Stories

This anthology of nostalgic dog tales celebrates the timeless virtues of loyalty, honor, friendship, and devotion. From Owney, the post office mongrel who traveled the world with as great a devotion to mailbags as any human postal carrier, to Wolf, the less-than-perfect collie who was not show quality but a born watchdog who thwarted a thief despite being poisoned, these stories are among the most moving and memorable you'll ever read.
Paperback, 160 pages. 0-8163-2045-4 US$12.99

Smoky, the Ugliest Cat in the World
and Other Great Cat Stories

The second installment in The Good Lord Made Them All series, this collection of memorable and heart-tugging feline tales will evoke laughter, tears, and wonder. Burned almost beyond recognition, a cat named Smoky with an iron will to live will blaze his way into your heart. In another story, a calloused physician takes pity on a badly wounded kitten and recaptures a lost love. And from the author's own life files, the story of the mysterious black cat named C.C. that brought comfort to the dying and grieving family members will leave its mark on your soul.
Paperback, 160 pages. 0-8163-2121-3 US$13.99

Order from your ABC by calling **1-800-765-6955,** or get online and shop our virtual store at **<www.adventistbookcenter.com>.**

- Read a chapter from your favorite book
- Order online
- Sign up for email notices on new products

Prices subject to change without notice.